the eBay
C⚛DE

the eBay
C⬤DE

The eBay Detective
Book Two

Charles A. Salter

TATE PUBLISHING
AND ENTERPRISES, LLC

Published by Tate Publishing & Enterprises, LLC
127 E. Trade Center Terrace | Mustang, Oklahoma 73064 USA
1.888.361.9473 | www.tatepublishing.com

Tate Publishing is committed to excellence in the publishing industry. The company reflects the philosophy established by the founders, based on Psalm 68:11,
"The Lord gave the word and great was the company of those who published it."

Book design copyright © 2013 by Tate Publishing, LLC. All rights reserved.
Cover design by Allen Jomoc
Interior design by Caypeeline Casas

Published in the United States of America

ISBN: 978-1-62510-803-6
Fiction / War & Military
12.11.30

Author's Note

All the dated radiation accidents, attacks, suicides, and other incidents in this volume are real and occurred just as described.

Prologue

Late in the evening, Army Specialists John Byrnes, age twenty-seven, and Richard McKinley, twenty-two, and Navy Electrician's Mate Richard Legg, twenty-six, entered the SL-1 nuclear power reactor building situated in a desert forty miles west of Idaho Falls, Idaho. Two of them would never be seen alive again, and one would disappear for a time.

The Stationary Low-power Reactor Number One was an experimental US Army project to develop small, self-contained power and heat generators for undersized and remote military facilities such as isolated radar sites. The mission that night required the men to restart the nuclear chain reaction after it had been turned off for several days to complete routine maintenance.

The thirteen-ton reactor vessel was diminutive by industry standards, and Legg stood on top of it as McKinley watched nearby, and Byrnes endeavored to maneuver the central control rod. Deep in the core of the reactor lay the ferociously powerful nuclear fuel, enriched to such a degree that it constantly spit the subatomic particles known as neutrons in all directions, with each atomic fission releasing heat energy and more radiation. Each fission, when uncontrolled, tended to trigger a cascade of other atoms to split as the stray neutrons struck them in turn.

When controlled, this process led to a self-sustaining chain reaction that produced intense heat to boil water into steam, which led into a turbine to produce electrical power. At the same time, the superheated water leaving the vessel and being replaced with fresh water served to cool the reactor and leave its temperature within tolerable limits, much like a car radiator system with liquid coolant. When properly placed fully in the midst of the nuclear fuel, the central control rod kept the chain reaction under control by safely absorbing most of the spare neutrons and preventing them from splitting too many other atoms. As the control rod was increasingly withdrawn, more and more nuclear material would be exposed to stray neutrons. The increased fission reactions produced a rapid escalation in heat and nuclear energy to produce dramatically more power.

That night Byrnes attempted to reconnect the eighty-four-pound central control rod to the automated assembly, which ensured it remained at the right height during operations to prevent power losses or surges. During the months of training required before these men began their work within the reactor area, it was drilled into them repeatedly that they should never raise the central control rod more than four inches from the base of the nuclear pile. To do so would invite disaster, risking loss of control over the chain reaction—a criticality incident, in nuke-speak.

Four inches didn't give Byrnes much maneuvering room to reattach the rod to the assembly. The other two men watched silently as he struggled, sweat no doubt forming on his forehead.

Then the unthinkable happened.

Winter 2003

In Frederick, Maryland, lying in a warm bed, US Army Major Brad Stout was definitely out of uniform. Way out.

He rolled away from his fiancée, Mary Lou Boudreaux, panting, exhausted but feeling ten feet tall. He turned back toward her, his smile framed by sweat. She had small beads of sweat too, but on her they looked like glistening raindrops on her alabaster skin. The medium-length brown hair framed her lovely oval face—one dominated by enormous blue eyes, full of life and fire, and rich full lips, whose kiss always turned him to putty.

"My sweet Cajun princess, what is it about pregnancy that makes you so completely voluptuous and insatiable?"

"I dunno." She smiled back. "But you better enjoy it while you can. Another couple of months and I'll be too big with the twins to do much of anything…this athletic, anyway."

"I don't like the sound of that." He leaned over and kissed her moist and tender lips. "You mean to say you're going to abandon me when the little ragin' Cajuns join us?"

"Well." She leaned over and whispered in his ear, "There's more than one way to clean the pirogue."

"Yeah, but I like *this* way."

"Tough, toadie. The owl master can't always get his favorite tree."

"Hmm, I'm beginning to sense one of the drawbacks of fatherhood."

"Drawbacks? Don't worry about that. Cajun girls always take care of their men folk first. Take my mother, Josephine, for instance."

"Do I have to?"

"Have to what?"

"Take your mother?"

She curled her lip in mock exasperation. "Look, I know it's going to be tough having my parents hang around for a couple of weeks, but they want to be here for the wedding. And it's about time you guys met each other."

"That reminds me—I'm supposed to pick up your father at the airport this evening, right?"

"Oh, nooo! *We* have to pick him up together. And I'm driving. I don't want you getting distracted when he starts in and have an accident."

"Starts in? What is that supposed to mean?"

"I can't describe it. But you'll see what I mean when it happens."

Oh, great…meeting the porcupine king for the first time was going to be tough enough already. But this sounds downright ominous. "I still don't understand why your mom isn't flying up with him."

"Because she doesn't believe people can fly."

"Doesn't believe? Her own husband is flying up."

"She doesn't believe he can do it either. She's never left St. Martin Parish, the deep bayou country, before in her life. We're lucky she's willing to come up from Louisianne on a train. You watch when she gets here a couple of days later. She won't rest until she sees Dad is really here in the flesh and not just a bayou ghost."

Charming. This is going to be one heckuva couple of weeks. "I'm nervous enough about the wedding as it is, and you're driving me right off the Richter scale talking like that."

"Nervous? Why should you be nervous? Aren't you getting what you always wanted?" She licked her lips as if preparing for more action and nestled closer to him under the sheets.

He put his arm around her and pressed against her warm flesh. "Oh, yeah. No doubt about that. I'm not nervous about formalizing our commitment and declaring our love. I'm just nervous about getting everything at work done in time so I can make it to the wedding."

"You better make it to the wedding!"

"Well if the AFRRI commander had his way, I'd be in Siberia instead. So don't blame me if he pulls something else at the last minute. He's been a total bear ever since our adventure with the dirty bomb terrorists last fall when I killed the ringleader in the cobalt-60 radiation exposure room at the lab."

Her lovely blue eyes lost their focus on him for a moment, as if powerful memories tugged at her consciousness. She involuntarily shivered, and he drew her even closer.

Her eyes refocused, and her dimples broke out as she smiled. "Don't you ever go risking your life with radiation terrorists again. The twins and I can't risk losing you now. All right? Never again!"

He suddenly felt glum and looked away, burying his face in the tangle of her fresh-smelling brown hair strewn over the pillow. *If only Mary Lou knew what I was tracking on eBay right now, she wouldn't have said that. She would have recognized a self-fulfilling prophecy in the making.*

Right now only Brad knew what he was up to in his military mission to keep an eye on all things radioactive on eBay. He hadn't yet even told the commander of the Armed Forces Radiobiology Research Institute—or AFRRI—because it appeared to him that a shadowy group was dealing with radioactive materials on eBay in code. Since the incident of the dirty bomb last autumn, eBay had changed their rules and no longer allowed the selling and buying of radioactive elements unless they were clearly in very small, sub-lethal quantities—samples of uranium and radium for science experiments and to test radiac devices, for instance. Brad wasn't sure whether he had cracked the code correctly or not, but if he had, someone was trying to bring the nightmarish SL-1 horror back to life, something all rad experts had come to believe had been dead and buried for four decades. Even…even the infamous "radiation hand of death," if that were possible. It seemed inconceivable, so Brad wanted to make sure he knew what he was talking about before telling the commander.

After a quick shower, Brad went downstairs in his skivvies to make some Salada green tea, glad that he and Mary Lou had the house to themselves for a few weeks while his older sister, Victoria, toured the German Rhineland and other parts of Europe with her new job as a travel writer. She had finally given up trying to find a position as a tech writer in the Frederick area and had never had success getting a job as a music professor either. But as a member of the *American Society of Journalists and Authors*, she jumped at the opportunity to become a travel writer when the position was listed on their confidential members-only website.

In a way, Brad wished he were on that trip. When Victoria showed him all the pictures from the Rhine River cruise line—the gorgeous and cozy cruise ship, the magnificent cliffs on both sides, the majestic castles over-looking the water—he really wanted to join her…just as they had travelled to Germany together years earlier to tour Heidelberg, flying to Frankfurt and then taking the train to several tourist destinations along the way.

On the other hand, having Victoria out of the country while he and Mary Lou prepared for the wedding made their lives a bit easier. His sister's prediction that there could only be one mistress of the household was proving true. With the wedding fast approaching, Mary Lou gave up her apartment and moved in with the two siblings. Brad and Victoria owned equal shares of their house, which their mom had willed to them years ago. Victoria didn't want Brad to move out and leave her alone, yet neither did she want to cede household leadership to Brad's new fiancée. They were constantly at each other's throats that first couple of weeks, the aristocratic and often snooty Victoria versus the sweet girl-next-door Cajun who could go ragin' and scrappin' like a wild catamount at the first sign of an insult.

It was proving fortuitous that the two women were a few thousand miles apart for now. Brad didn't know what they would do when Victoria returned.

2

Brad went for one of his ten-mile runs late that afternoon. He exited their home on Gas House Pike just outside the city limits of Frederick, ran east along the pike for a few miles, then turned south on Boyers Mill Road then east onto Eagle Head Drive into the Lake Linganore section of New Market.

It was sunny out with a gorgeous blue sky framed by little wisps of clouds. It was also very cold, but with the body heat he produced running at his best army speed, he needed nothing more than a light jacket, an Old Navy cap with flaps over the ears, and his army wool glove inserts for his hands. As usual, ever since his encounter with the brood a few weeks earlier, he ran with an eye out for any kind of trouble, anyone suddenly coming up to confront him. It was one reason why he no longer ran in the dark like he used to, either first thing in the morning or after the end of a hard day's work.

The brood. How many were there? In his last adventure, he had been attacked by three. One Brad himself killed, another he helped the FBI capture, but that one was murdered in jail by one or more other unidentified brood members. The third Brad helped capture still sat in protective custody, because the FBI didn't want to lose their number one lead to the rest of the gang of dirty bomb terrorists.

But how many more were there operating in the Frederick region? He had picked up a few clues but didn't have much to go on. The Frederick brood had attacked him and earlier sneaked anthrax out of the biowarfare lab at Fort Detrick in downtown Frederick and mailed that around the country about a month after 9/11. A different brood had apparently killed at least one biowarfare defense scientist in Tennessee, and the man still in jail—formerly a casual friend to Brad but steady boyfriend of Victoria—spoke of a master brood, which apparently operated on a national level to maintain control over the scattered branches of their syndicate. Members of any or all of these could conceivably be after Brad if they knew the extent of his role in halting their dirty bomb production by tracking down their efforts to obtain radioactive materials and scientific know-how using eBay.

Brad ran up the hill on Eagle Head and passed lovely Lake Merle, surrounded by oak and maple trees with a restored Civil War homestead in red brick at the far end where the swans swam about in better weather. A thin layer of ice now lay across the lake, and Brad could see through the woods in every direction, since all the leaves had turned brown, red, or golden weeks earlier and fallen to the ground. He proceeded up the steep, long hill into the Balmoral section of Lake Linganore, this section built along the high ridge between the two lakes—Merle and the neighborhood's namesake lake.

How many in a brood? How many left in the Frederick area who have polluted eBay and would love to remove me from the face of the earth as revenge for trying to halt their malignant activities? A biologist who specialized in radiation biology at Johns Hopkins University, Brad knew nature boasted several kinds of broods, but they all varied in number. A brood of chicks may include only about half a dozen. A brood of wild turkeys out West might run up to a dozen or more.

But this syndicate brood bore no resemblance to chicks or turkeys. This was a brood of human pit vipers, and depending upon biological species, a viper brood could be as few as two individuals all the way up to eighty or more for the deadly fer-de-lance. Brad hoped that the number of humans in the terrorist brood in his region was no more than four. With three of those out of commission and at least one more operating in prison, that would mean no members left free in this area. *If only.*

Red streaks struggled to form in the sky as the sun wearily began to set. He glanced at his watch as he ran east on Balmoral along the crest of the ridge. He would need to turn around and head back soon if he were going to arrive at the house before dark. But he knew it was less than a quarter of a mile to the end of this road, and that point provided one of the most spectacular views in New Market. If he reached just the right spot, he could look left and watch the hill steeply descend over rock and scrub brush to the lovely and dark surface of Lake Linganore. But if he looked forward, he stood at the very top of the sheer cliff that plummeted to the old Susquehanna Indian caves at the bottom of the rock face.

Picking up speed now as the road leveled while traversing the ridge, he remembered the first time he had run to this area. It seemed so beautiful and peaceful that he stopped running that day years ago and walked to the edge for a better view. Suddenly the trail ended. It just stopped. If he hadn't been closely watching his path that day for snakes, he might have tripped and tumbled right over the edge. No railing, no warning signs, nothing. With all the trees on this end of the ridge and also on the next ridge on the other side of the narrow gorge formed by Linganore Creek, it was easy not to notice the sudden drop.

As it turned out on that first visit, he instead spotted a very narrow and steep, winding path crisscrossing a portion of the cliff by which he could safely reach the bottom on foot. He did so that day but was very mindful of the small critter-sized caves and openings that dotted the bluff like pock marks on a grizzled face. *A perfect place for a timber rattlesnake*, he had thought.

He never took that trail down the cliff again to visit the old Indian caves, though over the years he loved to run across the top of the ridge, enjoying a view growing more golden and breath-taking with every step. And he often ran the other route, which skipped the ridge and ended naturally at the base of the cliff, right at the cave mouth.

Not many cars on the ridge today, but something loud and mechanical began to roar up from behind him. The paved road lay very curved and narrow here, only about two-tenths of a mile from the end, so without looking back, Brad made a horizontal loop-the-loop off the road into a long driveway, intending to keep moving and return to the road behind the vehicle as it passed.

No dice. The white van, windowless except for the front windshield and door windows in front, abruptly stopped perpendicular to the driveway, scratching up the gravel as its brakes took hold.

Brad's heart seemed to speed up, even though he was only running in place at this moment. He looked both ways and decided to speed around the back of the van and head back home.

The van driver didn't seem to like that idea. As soon as Brad changed direction toward the rear, the driver threw his transmission into reverse and slammed the accelerator and then the brakes, shooting up gravel as he sped back ten feet and completely blocked that exit for Brad.

Without hesitation, Brad instantly changed direction and fled full speed around the front of the van and headed toward the end of the road at the cliff's edge.

The driver responded in kind, popping into forward gear and flooring it again.

But in the second it took the van to shift direction and pick up speed, Brad was flying a good eight to ten yards in the lead and hugging the side of the tree-lined road. The van could come along beside him, but if it suddenly propelled directly toward him, it would more likely hit solid wood rather than Brad.

Beginning to pant seriously for the first time in this run, Brad kept bobbing in and out among the trees along the roadside. He was glad he had his Smith and Wesson neck knife hanging from a chain around his neck. The sheath doubled as a loud whistle to call for help. The knife itself was small and light but included a three and a half inch, incredibly sharp blade.

"We want that diary," bellowed a deep voice from the half-open driver window of the van.

The diary! That could mean only one thing—the diary I used as bait to help catch the first brood member last fall. The World War II diary Brad had spent three thousand dollars to acquire on eBay, *Diary of an American Officer in Himmler's SS*.

The gravel road was ending now, and ahead lay just the open-foot trail in the nearly treeless patch at the very crest of the ridge. Brad raced for the edge, eyes on the ground to make sure he didn't trip and sail over the cliff's edge to certain death on the sharp rocks below.

The van driver, apparently intent on Brad, floored his vehicle again, seemingly intending to crush Brad before he could escape.

January 3, 1961

Pandemonium was about to spread at the National Reactor Testing Station in Idaho. About 9:00 p.m. at the SL-1 facility a security guard noted the radiation alarm beside him going off. It had malfunctioned before, and he assumed it was doing so again. He reset it.

It immediately went off again. He reset it again then called the instrument repair shop to inform them the monitor must be broken again.

It never even occurred to him that the alarm might be telling the truth.

9:01 p.m.

The heat detection alarm positioned above the roof of the reactor building sounded at the Station's fire department. A team of six rushed to investigate. The reactor building appeared normal and without damage…from the outside.

They entered the building, noting that all the radiation warning lights in the building were on. Immediately the radiation detectors they carried with them pegged—going straight to the top of the scale as far as their instruments could detect, signifying the actual radiation levels must be far higher…extraordinarily lethal with even a brief exposure. They were forced to retreat and report their findings.

9:17 p.m.

A radiation expert, a health physicist, and another fireman wearing protective equipment arrived to investigate. They made it as far as the stairs of the reactor building before radiation readings on their instruments forced them to turn back and escape the invisible but deadly radiation cloud.

Minutes later, a team equipped with instruments capable of more accurately reading high levels of radiation appeared and entered. They saw on their detectors readings of 500 röntgens per hour—a dose that would give an unshielded human a lethal dose in less than an hour. However, they wore full-body protective clothing so investigated long enough to see through a window into the reactor vessel room.

They were astonished at the devastation. As was revealed in the full investigation much later, for reasons unknown, Byrnes had withdrawn the central control rod an estimated twenty-six inches rather than the mandatory maximum of four. Normal operating power in the reactor was two hundred kilowatts, but in just four thousandths of a second, the power had surged to twenty billion watts (some ten thousand times as much) with a total loss of control over the neutron flux rate. The intense, nearly instantaneous nuclear force caused a steam explosion so powerful that the fuel and water vaporized in the heat, creating a force on the reactor head of ten thousand pounds per square inch and exploding the entire thirteen-ton reactor vessel into the air.

The rescue team did not know all those details upon their first glance into the reactor room, but they could tell instantly that something dreadful had occurred and had destroyed the entire system. There was no sign of the doomed operators, and with their remaining seconds of exposure time without risking their own lives dwindling, they hastily made their way back out to safety.

10:30 p.m.

Now that a criticality incident had been confirmed and the extent of the damage and intense radioactivity become finally clear, another rescue team was formed. Each volunteer was given a strict limit of one minute's exposure, sixty seconds to do or find what he could and then report back.

With this approach, the team was finally able to locate two of the three men on the floor, both horribly mutilated by the explosion, but one was still barely breathing. Other rescuers brought out on stretchers the dead Specialist Byrnes, the one who had manipulated the heavy control rod, and the barely alive Specialist McKinley, who had been standing apart from the vessel when it exploded.

"Where is Navy Electrician's Mate Richard Legg?" asked the team chief of the last stretcher-bearers out of the horror zone.

"I'm not sure."

"How can you not be sure? Did you see him or didn't you?"

"I don't know. I saw something...but I'm not sure if it was human."

Winter 2003

Brad ran east down Balmoral as fast as he could, straight for the precipice of the cliff.

Behind him the driver of the unidentified white van sped up to catch him and presumably run him over. The sun was starting to set in the west behind the driver, sending scarlet streaks across the sky, which might distract his concentration on what lay ahead beyond the target he aggressively pursued.

Brad headed for a young sapling near the very edge, one with a trunk diameter only a few inches thick, small enough for him to grasp with his hands. With his last few inches of earth under his feet, he twisted into an abrupt angle to the left as his feet flew over the edge, grasping the sapling with both hands and intending to rotate around it back to solid ground.

He could hear but not see the van plunging over the edge with a final snarl of tire tread on gravel.

For a second he felt disoriented, unable to see the car plunging some sixty feet to the jagged rocks below and unable to maintain his grasp on the tree trunk and spin without lacerating his hands on the bark. He gripped the trunk tighter to avoid scraping, but then he couldn't rotate as he might on a smooth fire pole, so his feet didn't quite regain terra firma. In fact, the young sapling began to bend under his weight, farther and farther out over the precipice.

He dangled there over the edge, looking down between his feet to watch the explosion, wondering if a stray door might careen like a bomb fragment right up into his body.

There was a horrible crashing sound and the screech of torn metal but no explosion. Didn't cars always explode on contact with the cliff bottom in countless movies? It wasn't going to happen in real life now that he needed it?

He tried to anchor his feet on a craggy ledge of rock but couldn't reach it. He looked down again and could now see what looked like a corpse—or what would soon become a corpse—with a bloody head protruding through the broken windshield on the driver's side.

On the passenger side someone was still alive enough to be struggling to open that partially crushed door.

Just then several roots of the sapling began to snap loose from their shallow mounting, one at a time. Brad had previously observed that bushes and even fairly large trees sometimes seemed to grow out of little more than solid rock along this cliff. Somehow their root tendrils found enough moisture in small patches of soil, leaf cake, and cracks in the rock to survive, but they weren't strongly anchored.

Mindless now of the pain in his hands as the tree sagged to a nearly horizontal position, he tried to propel himself down the trunk hand over hand toward the base.

Just as the main taproot gave way, he was able to grab a sharp rock atop the cliff and shift his weight to that. More lacerations, and his skinned hands really burned now.

From the edge he looked down to see a dark-clad figure struggling to escape the half-opened passenger door.

Brad grunted as he used all his strength to pull himself up and over the edge, hands aflame, Nike running shoes scrambling for a footing on anything that wouldn't give way.

Made it! He rolled onto his back, gasping for breath for only a second or two. Then he looked back over the edge.

The crash survivor looked dazed but also seemed to have mayhem on his mind. He wasn't trying to get away or help any buddies in the vehicle but had his eyes on Brad, looking some sixty feet up at him.

He's on foot and will need minutes to get up the cliff to me. I know where I am and all the shortcuts to depart the area before he can possibly get up high enough to see me again. But then he can just bide his time and look for me another day. This ends now. *Gotta take care of this brood guy once and for all. He can surrender, or he can fight, but he is not going to just walk away.*

Brad picked up the largest rock he could find—about the size of a soccer ball—and threw it straight at the burly man's head. He missed, of course, but his real intent was to keep the man on the defensive while Brad descended to him. Brad grabbed a pile of smaller rocks and kept tossing them as he weaved his way down the trail. More blood and pain in his hands, but he didn't want to give the dazed man a spare moment to formulate a plan.

The man disappeared into the mouth of the main Indian cave, and Brad made sure to hop off the bottom of the cliff trail at a spot where he could see the cave and not be surprised by the thug coming up behind him.

Brad could hear the babbling of Linganore Creek now, and he noted that the rocks in the gorge were either moist from the creek's mist or coated with a thin layer of slippery ice. *Gotta keep my feet on soil or tree roots and avoid those rocks!*

Brad could see the man now. Medium height, dark chinos, and a thick jacket. He appeared to be visually scanning the area near the van, perhaps looking for a firearm or other weapon lost in the crash. There was a big gash in the man's forehead, his thick hair matted with blood. His eyes looked a little bloodshot. He probably had a concussion, which could give Brad the edge in the hand-to-hand combat to come.

Brad noted the strewn wreckage of the van. It lay mostly in one piece but badly crushed. Shards of windshield glass of all sizes lay strewn about, and sharp pieces of torn doorframes, bumpers, and fenders protruded at crazy angles from the sides of the vehicle.

The man saw Brad now and growled like a feral beast, apparently trying to intimidate his foe while still desperately looking for a weapon—either a firearm now lost or a makeshift weapon such as a sharp branch.

"Do you want to surrender…or die?" Brad asked in the most menacing tone he could conjure up.

The man growled again and clenched his fists into giant battering rams.

In warrior mode now, Brad's attention focused on just one thing—how to take down this would-be killer, analyzing strengths and weaknesses, looking for an opening. They faced each other from a distance of about ten paces now. Brad noted the heavyset face and thick neck and wrists—all signs of a hardened fighter or gangster, but the man still looked dazed and disoriented, no doubt wishing he were better armed. Brad, on the other hand, had bleeding and burning palms but was otherwise unharmed and had the home-turf advantage of familiar territory. He knew, for instance, precisely what lay in the back of the Indian cave.

As Brad took his first step into the fighting circle, drawing out and brandishing his neck knife, the sound of approaching sirens burst through the background noise of the nearby stream. Someone must have seen or heard the crash and called for an ambulance.

The noise startled the man, but then his glance riveted onto something that lay a few feet from the passenger door. Brad instantly followed the angle of that gaze and locked onto the small and dark object, too. A small semi-auto pistol.

Both men broke toward it immediately, instinctively knowing that whoever reached it first would win this fight.

Brad kept his footsteps on soil, leaves, and fallen branches, but heedless of any risk, the gunsel plowed straight ahead over the wet, icy rocks. Suddenly he slipped, plunged forward with great force…right onto a two-foot spike of door frame.

He impaled himself right through the center of the chest, and Brad could see the bloody tip protruding out the back of his jacket. There was a final *unghh*, and then the body went limp.

The sirens were nearer now.

What to do? Brad hadn't laid a finger on the man. He hadn't really done anything but run for his life and throw a few rocks, none of which connected. If he waited for the police, he would no doubt be questioned as a material witness for hours…but then he would be late to help Mary Lou pick up her Cajun father flying in from Lafayette, Louisiana, in a couple of hours. And then *she* would be an enraged alligator ready to bite Brad's head off for missing the first meeting with his new father-in-law.

What good would it do to remain? He had left no fingerprints. He didn't recognize the men, nor did he really know anything about them. Suspecting he might be making a bad decision, he nevertheless took off, scrambling back up the trail and heading for home. But first he bent over and took a quick look at the pistol on the ground. A Makarov 9 mm, clearly the East German version (marked by a small circle in a square by the safety lever), the one used by the Stasi or Secret Police before the re-unification of Germany in 1990 some dozen years ago. Was this goon with the brood? With the now-dismantled Stasi? Or both?

Why did they want the old WWII spy diary that Brad bought on eBay and used to help catch the dirty bomber Cujo-man? The FBI had taken it as evidence when they arrested the perp. When Brad protested, the special agent said he could put in a claim to get it back after the trial and appeals all ended. That never happened, because Cujo-man was murdered in jail by someone from the brood. When Brad subsequently did put in a claim, it was denied, since Cujo-man had paid Brad for the diary. Though he never was able to take possession of it, it was ruled by the court as belonging to the deceased man's estate.

Brad had no idea where the diary was any more and had no way to get his hands on it.

Hmmm. What if the fourth brood member wasn't a prisoner, as I always assumed based on the newspaper report? What if he were a guard or another member of law enforcement at the jail? Another good reason for Brad not to attract too much police attention right now, though he had the uneasy feeling that skipping the crash scene would soon come back and bite him in the rear.

January 3, 1961

At the National Reactor Testing Station in Idaho, this was the most shocking development yet in a day with nothing but shocking developments.

"What do you mean you're not sure if it is human?" the exasperated rescue team chief asked the last stretcher-bearer out of the ruined nuclear reactor building.

The other two victims were mutilated but still clearly human; one still alive, though probably not for long.

The rescue volunteer's eyes were wide, and he gasped for gulps of fresh air as he spoke after racing through the building at top speed for his allotted sixty seconds of radiation exposure time, helping to carry a heavy load while dressed in massive gear.

"I don't know what to tell you, Chief! The other two guys were on the floor. No sign of the third man on the floor, on the furniture, not anywhere you would expect. So I looked up, and there was a bloody smear on the ceiling right above the reactor vessel. At least I think it was blood, but with all the molten fuel and reactor bits flung out by the explosion, I couldn't be sure without getting closer… maybe up on a ladder or something."

The chief grimaced and felt something twist in the bottom of his stomach. Had the man been flattened like road kill under a Mack truck but into the ceiling by the force of the explosion? He would have to check out this lead, but right now he had bigger problems. The two recovered bodies were giving off frighteningly high radiation readings. The nuclear criticality had turned their very flesh into potent emitters of radiation. This had never happened before in the history of nuclear science and radiation accidents. Nothing in all his many years of training and experience had prepared him for this. Handling the body of the dead man or trying to aid the dying man could make victims of all of them, the whole rescue team—anyone coming near. They would all get a lethal dose in less than an hour if they remained in the building or anywhere near these bodies or the wreckage of the reactor vessel.

6

At the sprawling Baltimore-Washington International Airport complex, Brad and Mary Lou waited by the exit from the secure area, scanning the arriving throng for her father.

Earlier upon returning from his run, Mary Lou had helped clean and bandage his damaged hands. When she asked how it happened, he decided not to tell her about the white van chasing him and the men who were killed. Brad was still processing this information himself and trying to make sense of it all. He saw no reason to bring her into this dark space today and dampen the entire experience of reuniting with family and sharing in the joy of next week's wedding. He just muttered something about scraping his hands in a fall against a tree trunk, which was the truth as far as it went.

Waiting at the noisy airport, suddenly Mary Lou perked up and literally jumped a couple of inches into the air. Her expression brightened, and the veins in her neck stood out. "There! There he is!" She started to wave excitedly, her grin spreading from ear to ear.

Brad looked into the throng of maybe five hundred approaching people. "Where? Which one?"

Without looking down, she whispered, "The handsome one, silly! Right there!" She waved and squealed with delight.

Brad scanned the crowd again, noting dozens of handsome men around middle age, many of them looking toward his fiancée. He was way used to that. She was so gorgeous and shapely that everywhere they went men of all ages, even boys, eagerly watched her.

"I don't see him!"

She broke off her visual lock-on just a second to glance at Brad. "It's the good-looking, cool guy! There's only one! Are you blind?"

Brad held his tongue until he could see, breaking from the crowd and waving back, a fiftyish man with a thick head of dark hair tinged with a bit of grey at the temples and a tall, thin, muscular body like a fisherman or manual laborer might have. Brad felt like he had emerged from a time machine to see himself in about twenty years. The thought gave him a queasy feeling.

As soon as the man emerged from the secure zone, Mary Lou burst forward and flung herself on him, her eyes moist, holding him tight. Brad held back a couple of minutes to allow them a private moment.

Then, arm around Dad's waist, she brought him over to the pillar where Brad stood. "Daddy, I want you to meet my fiancée, Brad Stout, US Army major!"

Dad grimaced. "A field grade officer, huh? Never had much use for them. I was an NCO in the National Guard 256th Infantry Brigade. You ever see the film *Southern Comfort?*"

Yeah, Brad had seen it. What a reference! The one about a squad of national guardsmen in the Louisiana bayous being attacked and gradually killed off by local Cajuns.

Mary Lou looked cross. "Daddy, behave yourself!" she chided.

"I didn't mean nothing by it. I was just trying to tell him I played one of the extras in that film when I was a young man. Remember where they butcher the hog back at the village near the end? That was me in the background there."

"Daddy," said Mary Lou, hands on hips, arms akimbo. "Brad doesn't want to hear about your one claim to fame. Now come on and make nice."

"Well, it's the truth. I never had much use for commissioned officers. I knew a couple of majors I would have liked to choke with my bare hands."

This is not going very well. Brad started moving toward the exit, trying to get them away from the noisy, milling crowd to where they could converse better.

His fiancée glared at her pere.

"Okay, my petite cher. Laissez le bon temps rouler." Dad grinned.

Mary Lou interrupted, "That means—"

"Let the good times roll," said Brad. "I know. I took high school French."

Dad grinned again and reached out his hand toward Brad. "Shake my hand, son, and let's start over."

Brad brought up his hands like a holdup victim to show them both in bandages. He shrugged apologetically.

Dad frowned. "I always say you can only get to know a man by—"

Mary Lou broke in. "By how he shakes your hand. I know, Daddy, but Brad got lacerations all over both hands just a couple of hours ago. I don't want him to start bleeding again."

Dad looked from Brad's hands to his eyes. "Get into a death fight, son? I'll bet the other fellows got the worst of it—am I right?"

Brad chuckled nervously. *Right now I think I'd rather be back there fighting for my life than going through this.* "Say, Dad, is that what I should call you, or would you rather Pierre?"

"Not Py-*err*—I ain't from Paree. Say it like Pee-Aire, son, like you mean it, or just call me Dad. Don't say Daddy, though, that's just for my own kids. D'accord?"

"Oui." To Mary Lou, Brad said, "He's got other kids? You never told me you had any siblings."

"I didn't want to scare you off from marrying me."

"What's *that* supposed to mean?"

"Don't worry. They're not coming to the wedding. You won't have to deal with them."

Glumly, Brad tried to change the topic. "Got any check-in luggage, Dad, or should we head for my car?"

"Never carry luggage, son. Don't need it. Just carry what I wear on my back and wash it once a week…whether it needs it or not."

Brad now led the way through the tunnel, which reeked of spent diesel fuel, over the street traffic into the airport central garage.

"He's kidding," broke in Mary Lou. "Usually he wears two outfits when he starts out traveling and then alternates them during the trip." She turned to her father. "Daddy, if you don't watch yourself, you're going to make Brad think you're a Cajun coonass."

"Quelle dommage, ma belle fille. But wait till he meets Ma."

Mary Lou grabbed Brad's right arm and moved close to his ear. "Yeah, sweetie pie. You think Daddy is something, just wait till you meet Ma!"

"Speaking of Ma," said Dad while patting his daughter's baby bump, "Son, it has come to my attention that you been gigging my little girl pretty regular-like for a while now. Before the priest done made it official and all."

Brad was speechless.

Mary Lou slapped Dad's hand. "You little terror, you. Taisez-vous! Firmez le bouche!"

Dad doubled over in mock pain at her tap but giggled. "Just joshing you, son. Everybody needs a little now and then. I know that as well as the next man." He leaned over closer and lowered his voice. "Still 'n again, when Ma gets here I wouldn't do no gigging, leastways not till after the weddin'. Why once I seen Ma cut 'em right off a gator whilst it was still twitching after I shot it in the haid with mah 12-gauge. Used her genuine Jim Mustin Cajun knife."

"Shush, Daddy." Turning to Brad, she said, "He's just polecatting you again. Ma wouldn't hurt a living creature like that…leastways not an animal."

"Shoot! To Ma everything's an animal. Ma's still got that mummified alligator penis on her charm necklace. Right next to the chicken's foot. In fact, they look quite a bit alike."

"Daddy, for the last time!" Turning to Brad, she explained, "Now you know why everyone back home calls Dad the porcupine king, 'cause he's prickly all over but still kinda cute and cuddly."

Dad smiled sheepishly, trying to look modest.

Brad thought he would throw up.

February 20, 1999

A welder working at the Yanango, Peru, hydroelectric power station about three hundred miles east of Lima completed an important weld and then waited for the radiographer to get an X-ray to verify there were no cracks or fissures.

Somehow the iridium-192 pigtail that produced the gamma rays for the picture became separated from the camera and fell to the ground. As he was about to leave the area, the welder noticed the shiny metallic twist of wire lying in the dust. He didn't know what it was, but it looked important—maybe even valuable—so he picked it up with his bare hand and placed it in the right rear pocket of his jeans. It sat there for several hours while he completed his shift and rode the mini-bus home for half an hour with about a dozen people, all of whom he was unintentionally irradiating.

At some point his right thigh began to hurt. He complained to his wife, took off his trousers to show her the sensitive area, and she noticed a broad, reddening patch. While he went to the local doctor, who advised him the problem was likely a spider or insect bite, the welder's wife and children sat near or hung around the jeans he had left on the floor with the pigtail still in the pocket.

February 21, 1999

Having unsuccessfully tried to use his camera on his next mission, the radiographer soon realized his radiological source was missing. He scoured the immediate area and found nothing. Carrying his radiation meter with him, he went to the welder's house, where he got high radiation readings.

The radiographer asked the man to produce the highly radioactive wire, and he complied. The expert, knowing how deadly the source was, asked the welder to throw it into the street. The radiographer then covered it with a rock to provide shielding and then called in the authorities to properly recover the dangerous pigtail and screen all the possibly exposed people for medical treatment.

They took the welder and his entire family to the Lima National Cancer Hospital as soon as possible.

February 22, 1999

A huge blister began to form on the welder's right leg, right where the buttock meets the thigh, surrounded by a spreading area of redness.

Shortly thereafter, blood tests revealed plummeting immunity as the radiation damage continued to kill off the man's protective lymphocytes and other cellular defenses.

March 1, 1999

Gradually but inexorably over the next few weeks, the right leg swelled, the blister turned into an ulcerated area, and the skin began to die and slough off. The pain in parts of the leg grew intense, and he needed continuous morphine, while in other parts the nerves grew numb and began to die.

Due to the loss of immunity, super infection by opportunistic microorganisms set in, despite all the treatments tried at the hospital. Infection soon led to fever.

The area of ulceration and necrosis began to spread to both halves of the buttocks and to the scrotum. It soon became clear that the ferocious level of radiation exposure sustained that first day was leading to progressive damage to a number of internal organs such as the stomach as well.

April 13, 1999

The fingers of the right hand, the one which had touched the rad source, began to turn green and then black.

Red blood cells were dying now in such numbers that he required blood transfusions.

May 28, 1999

As the ulceration and necrosis continued to spread despite all their best efforts, the Peruvian doctors realized they may soon lose their patient. They sent him to Paris, France, to receive more advanced care at the Percy Hospital, where some victims of previous international radiation accidents had been saved in recent years. Three days later he underwent surgery to have the tracts of necrotic or dead tissue removed.

August 16, 1999

The area of cellular death and organ destruction continued to spread despite several lesser surgical attempts to debride the area throughout the summer. Radical surgery of the right leg, hip, and buttock area was tried next. They had to give the victim a colostomy due to all the internal damage in the pelvic area.

October 17, 1999

By this time internal damage was progressing, and the remaining leg also began to dissolve into ulcerations. Realizing that their most advanced treatments weren't working, the French team decided to send the victim back to Peru, presumably so he could die at home with his family.

8

Back at the house, Brad offered to get his father-in-law a drink.

"Got any corn liquor, son? You know, moonshine?"

"Nope, Dad. No shine. But I've got some corn liquor that's been properly aged in charred, oaken casks. Up in these parts we call it bourbon."

The older man gave a hearty laugh. "So you can dish it out too, huh? I like that. If you don't have anything made in ol' Louisiane, such as Old New Orleans Rum, then I am partial to aged bourbon, especially Makers Mark. Something about that dollop of red wax used to seal 'em. Reminds me of Jean Lafitte, the pirate, buried treasure, and the above-ground cemeteries in old New Orleens."

"Oh," Brad continued to tease. "You'd like to be a swashbuckler, slicing and dicing your way up and down the Gulf Coast. Blood on your cutlass and blood in the water."

Dad nodded, grinning. "My pa named me after Jean's older brother, Pierre."

"Bet you like your whiskey neat—no ice, just like in the old days."

"Yup."

"Bout three fingers worth?"

"That'll do for a start. But you may as well leave the bottle."

Brad returned with the drinks, a mug of steaming green tea for himself.

Dad took a long pull off his straight whiskey and smacked his lips. "Sweet rattlesnake claws, but that is good! Thanks, son."

Brad nodded.

Dad took one look at Brad's beverage, and his upper lip curled in disgust. "Not much of a drinker, are you?"

"I have a snoot now and then. But right now, I'm not in the mood."

"What are ye in a mood fer?"

Uh oh.

"Gettin' me outta the house so you can have a go at Mary Lou?"

"Da-AD," Brad said, lowering the tone on the second half of the syllable. "I just want to talk and get to know you better."

The older man laughed. "Not much to know. I'm just a typical, regular Cajun through and through. I can go ta sleep in my pirogue out in the middle of the bayou with nuttin' but moonlight as my blanket, kiss the stars good night, and wake up 'n wrassle alligators all the next day. Pick my teeth with a mirleton and sweeten my breath with astringent persimmons. Why I can climb a magnolia with my eyes closed, leap atop the next-door oak, and slide down the moss inta da bayou and sink to da bottom for half a day lak Merrow the Cajun swampsprite. Comb my hair with copperheads, shine my shoes with water moccasins, and swab out my ears with cottonmouths. Why, I can—"

"Certainly fling the Cajun BS," broke in Brad.

"Dinner, guys!" yelled Mary Lou.

"And I can eat my weight in crawdads…uncooked. And shed 'em out the other end still snappin' at each other with their big, red claws."

Mary Lou appeared at the door. "Dadd-ee! Time for the porcupine king to take a break and come eat."

Dad stood up and drained his whiskey glass. "Why I can tickle my fancy with porcupine quills, drink any seven dry-landers under the bar, barrel 'em up in an empty whiskey cask, and carry 'em home with one hand."

Dad started heading for the dining room, a wee bit unsteady in his gait. "That's just the Cajun in me, boy."

"Is there anything you *can't* do, Dad?" Brad smirked.

"Can't…can't seem to keep the womenfolk happy. No man I know can do that for more than a bit at a time. But I reckon that's their problem, not mine. Whaddya think, sweet baby girl?"

"Daddy," said Mary Lou, "I think you shouldn't drink on an empty stomach." She reached up on tiptoe and kissed him gently on the chin. "Now firmez la bouche, and keep it closed, 'cepting when you're stuffing it with my excellent shrimp creole."

Dad made a show of pretend-zipping his mouth with his fingers and winked at his daughter. But two seconds later he started in again. "Why I can beat a dead horse and bring it back to life! I can drain the Mississippi River with one big gulp, take two steps left into God's country and spew out seventeen more bayous…without stopping for a breath! I can chew up a pine tree and spit out a Christmas tree complete with decorations and all the presents for the chilluns. I can…can…umm, that smells good, pretty girl." Dad sat down and almost missed the edge of his chair.

Brad followed him to the table. *This is going to be one long, unending two weeks!*

$$\times$$

The doorbell rang. Brad opened the door to see two men in sheriff's deputy uniforms.

"Major Stout?" asked the older one.

"Yes, sir. What can I do for you?"

"I'm Deputy Carlisle, and this is Deputy Lancer. We'd like to ask you some questions. May we come in?"

Brad ushered the men into the parlor, where they could be relatively private, but through the open doorway he could still see Dad in the other room no more than fifteen feet away.

"What would you like to know?"

"Major Stout, can you tell us where you were about 3:30 p.m. this past Tuesday?"

"Of course. I was out for my usual ten-mile run."

"And do you recall your route?"

"Sure. Back and forth along Gas House Pike, up and down Boyer's Mill, in and out of Lake Linganore."

"Major Stout, are you aware that the army has a DNA identification program?"

"Of course. I had to give a sample about a year ago and sign an acknowledgement."

"Well, then, is there anything you'd like to tell us about the ridge along Balmoral in Lake Linganore?"

"Certainly. That's a lovely area. I've been running up there for many years now. That's probably my favorite spot in this region reachable by foot."

"Sir, I don't think you are catching my drift. Or perhaps you are trying to be clever. Maybe too clever for your own good. Let me be more blunt. Would you tell us how fresh samples of your blood got up there on the ridge Tuesday?"

"No problem." He held up his bandaged hands for them to see. "You know, there's no fence or safety rail or signs up there or anything, and I almost slipped over the edge. I had to grab a sapling up there to get my balance, and the rough bark tore up my hands pretty badly."

Carlisle wrote something in a notebook and Lancer, the much younger man, continued.

"Yet you've been going up there for years. You said so yourself. Wouldn't you know where the edge was by now and how far you could go safely?"

Brad froze and could hear his own heartbeat. He struggled for the right words.

Lancer continued. "You wouldn't know anything about a white van up on the ridge that day would you?"

Brad hesitated a second too long. "Yeah, that's why I got so close to the edge. I thought I saw a white van down in the gorge."

Carlisle broke back in. "You wouldn't happen to know *why* it ran right off the top of the ridge and crashed, now, would you?"

Brad dodged. "Like I said, it's pretty dangerous up there. I think the county should put up some signs."

"I think you know that the county has no responsibility for the roads up in Lake Linganore. That's a private development."

The younger deputy broke in. "Major Stout, you're not giving us much to go on. Any idea why your blood was on some of the rocks at the bottom of the gorge?"

"Well, sure, when I nearly fell, I grabbed at everything I could reach—the sapling, but it started to give way, then the rocks, roots, anything I could reach. Some of the rocks pulled loose, and I could hear them crashing to the ground below."

"So you don't know anything about the three men in the van?"

Three men. Oh, no. I only saw two dead. Must have been a third in the van the whole time I was there. "No, I never saw three men in the van."

"Yeah," said the junior deputy. "One crashed through the windshield and died instantly. One managed to exit the vehicle but strangely enough impaled himself on a spare spike of metal. But I don't suppose you can tell us how that happened?"

Brad shook his head. "And the third?"

"He's in intensive care. In a coma. But if he comes out of it and talks, I have a feeling we might want to talk to you again."

Brad shrugged and managed a nervous smile.

After the deputies left, Dad and Mary Lou stood in the open doorway to the front room; she looking confused and dazed.

A light of excitement danced in Dad's eyes, though. He slapped his thigh in amusement. "I *knew* it. I knew you got yourself a killer, cherie. I seen it in his eyes when I first caught sight of them in the airport. The blood lust. First thought he had it in for me, but that didn't make no sense. We're family now. But I seen it in your eyes. You know how to kill."

"Of course, he can kill, Daddy," broke in Mary Lou, consternation now mingling with what looked like pride. "He's an army officer, for Pete's sake! You know he killed that terrorist at the nuke place last fall and saved us all!"

"Well, sure, but now the po-leece is after him! Gollee, we got ourselves an outlaw in the family. A goodness sakes for real *outlaw*. Wait'll I tell Ma! She'll be tickled pink! Whoo-wee!"

9

What Brad had discovered on eBay was too important to wait for the next regular staff meeting. He made an appointment with the commanding officer of AFRRI to meet in the man's office.

Brad weaved his way through the labyrinth of heavyset, oddly angled, windowless corridors, walls made thick enough to contain an explosion or halt the spread of radiation in the event of an accidental or terrorist release. He trotted from the secure entrance past the nuclear reactor, downstairs to the executive suite where the commander's office, that of the executive officer, and also that of the lab's scientific director ringed a little waiting room with a few chairs and military magazines strewn about.

After just a minute's wait, the frazzled secretary, who always struggled mightily to juggle simultaneously the schedules of all the leadership, ushered him into Colonel Fukioki's office.

Ever since Brad fought to the death last autumn with the brood's terrorist leader in the cobalt-60 radiation exposure room, creating a nationwide split in the nuclear science community between those who blamed the commander for a scandal and those who considered Brad a hero for thwarting a nuclear terrorist plot, Brad had been on the man's crap list. Brad had been working on the Nuclear Regulatory Commission's paperwork ever since to explain exactly what happened and how Brad had managed, at great risk to his own life, to keep the public from any radiation exposure or harm.

The army colonel, a short and wiry Asian with little hair left, scowled at Brad as he entered. Brad didn't like being on the outs with the man, but Brad knew the man stuck to military rules and wouldn't screw him over in an illegal way just to be a vengeful jerk. Meanwhile, he had put in for a transfer, but every place that might need someone with his precise set of scientific and military skills seemed to share in the same difference of opinion. For every leader who wanted him at a given place, there was another who considered him scandalous and a loose cannon. For now, Brad was stuck at AFRRI—unless he decided to resign his commission and leave the army. But he hadn't even considered that option yet.

"So what have you found on eBay this time, Major?" asked the commander, pointing at the conference table for Brad to sit and moving over himself. Already at the table sat Navy Captain Pulowski, the head of the lab's radiation department and manager of all its rad sources.

Brad sat down, nodding at the captain, and then looked at the colonel. "Sir, you remember the SL-1 criticality incident of 1961?"

"Of course. Every rad expert learns about that one in the first semester. That's the one and only one where the bodies of the victims became such potent radiation emitters themselves that they had to be buried in lead-lined coffins with concrete shields and with extra concrete shielding atop the earth."

"Not all of them," interjected the captain.

"Are you referring to the body parts that were so intensely radioactive that they had to be removed and buried separately in a special radioactive waste dump?"

"Exactly," said Pulowski. "The hand of the man who was manipulating the central control rod, which was right over the reactor fuel when the vessel blew, became such an intense emitter that even the gold in his watch turned radioactive. Some of those body parts were giving off as much as fifteen hundred rads per hour…enough to deliver a lethal dose to someone exposed to them in under fifteen minutes."

"The radioactive hand of death," broke in Brad. "Then there was the guy standing on the reactor lid who was blown into the ceiling by the force of the explosion. In fact, one of the shield plugs burst from the reactor vessel's lid, impaled him right through the groin, and pinned him to the ceiling." Brad shuddered.

Pulowski added, "It took them days to get the body down, because it and the reactor room were so highly radioactive. It took five successive pairs of men, each allowed only about a minute's exposure time in that nightmarish room, using long poles with hooks on the end to finally scrape and pull the flattened remains loose. Nearly eight hundred people involved in the rescue and the eighteen-month cleanup operations were exposed to dangerous levels of radiation…though none of them received a fatal dose."

Colonel Fukioki asked, "But all that was over forty years ago. How is that relevant now?"

Brad responded, "It seems unbelievable in hindsight, but that area where they buried the remains of the reactor—some one hundred thousand cubic feet of radioactively contaminated material and the super-radioactive body parts—was not properly secured by capping the burial ground until just three years ago in 2000. Prior to that, the buried material was so hot they were getting radiation readings even above ground."

"So what? That is not surprising. But there was no threat to the public, since that was in an isolated area, completely fenced off with warning signs and everything."

Brad shook his head. "But if I am interpreting the code in several recent eBay auctions correctly, someone apparently broke into that area between 1962 and 2000 and recovered thousands of curies of radioactive material and—I'm not joking—the radioactive hand of death."

"You mean?"

"Yes. I think we have another dirty bomber on our hands."

✕

Brad turned into his driveway off Gas House Pike and noticed immediately that something was wrong. A huge blaze dominated the skyline where his house should be.

Heart thumping, he sped the hundred yards to see that his two-story brick dwelling was in no danger, but there was an enormous bonfire roaring no more than twenty yards from the front door and sending countless clouds of bright sparks rising up into the cold night sky. A strange man-like thing leapt and danced on the other side of the blaze. His head appeared to be covered in a huge grey bush, and he wore green tattered clothes like some kind of seasick Peter Pan. The creature emitted a noise like a kazoo humming, and both hands spun loud noisemakers. Other than appearing as the leader of an escaped band of mental patients, he seemed harmless enough.

Brad parked and dashed to the front door to see if he could find out what was going on.

Someone who looked an awful lot like Mary Lou met him at the doorway. Only this person wore an owl mask covering both eyes and sported a clump of some grayish mass pinned to the top of her head. There was likewise a clump of the grayish fibers taped to the doorframe above Brad. This female personage was also dressed in torn green clothes and spun loud noisemakers in both hands.

"A belated Merry Cajun Christmas to you, Brad!" she exclaimed, eyes dancing with the reflected light of the flickering fire behind him. "La la la la!" she sang loudly.

"What the heck?" asked Brad.

"Ma and Pa wanted us to go down to St. Martinville for Christmas, but we couldn't because of your NRC paperwork, so we decided to have a late celebration up here! *Surprise!*"

"I'm surprised, all right. That's putting it mildly! What's that crap on your head?"

"Spanish moss, of course! Daddy collected a pile from the oak trees back home before he left and smuggled it up here. You never even noticed the bag he had under his coat when we picked him up at the airport."

"So Ma is here now, too?"

"Naw. We're not sure when she's getting here, but PawPaw Noel didn't want to wait any longer. He wanted to do it while there is still plenty of snow on the ground."

"PawPaw Noel?"

"Yeah, the guy you drylanders call Father Christmas. Most Cajuns call him Papa Noel, but in my family it's always been PawPaw Noel."

"So who's the old coot leaping about like an oversized gnome by the fire?"

"Daddy, of course! He's in his PawPaw Noel get up!" She turned toward her father and yelled, "PawPaw Noel! Come meet Brad!"

In his lunatic outfit, Dad gamboled over, looking as much like a chimp in green as a man. As he drew near, Brad could see the head was covered in thick moss held in place with ribbons, bobby pins, and rubber bands. Streaks of several colors of lipstick ran amok all over his face.

"So, Dad, why the big fire?"

"Who is this *dad* you speak of? I am PawPaw Noel!"

"Okay, PawPaw Noel, I'll play along. Where did you get the wood for this huge bonfire?"

"I didn't get it. I think this here youngun's daddy got it…borrowed it from those woods up yonder."

"Those woods? That's marked, 'Keep out. Private property.' You can get fined for tramping around up there and taking stuff."

"No one can fine PawPaw Noel on baby Jesus day! Besides, I didn't take it—this here youngun's daddy must have."

"Why a bonfire anyway?"

"In Cajun country everyone builds a big bonfire to show PawPaw Noel the way to their house. Otherwise they won't get any presents, that's why!"

"Oh, so Santa—I mean, PawPaw Noel—flies in with his reindeer only to the lit-up homes?"

"Not reindeer—alligators. PawPaw Noel has eight alligators harnessed to his flying river boat."

"So I suppose the eight alligators are led by Rudolph, the red-nosed alligator?"

Mary Lou broke in. "Of course not, silly. They're led by Nicolette, the alligator whose green eyes shine bright and guide Noel's river boat this night."

"Oh, that song sounds familiar. I'll bet it starts with 'Nicolette, the green-eyed alligator, had very shiny eyes, and if you ever saw them, you would even say they cried.'"

"*No*, Brad, that sounds silly. You've got the tune all wrong."

"Well, let me get inside before you tell me more. It's freezing out here."

"Close your eyes first. You're standing under moss, you know."

Oh, I get it. It's like standing under mistletoe, and you get a kiss. He complied, puckering his lips slightly and waiting for some action. Suddenly he smelled something really gross, perhaps a goat cheese that had been left in the sun for a couple of weeks, and something sharp like a toothpick lightly pricked his upper lip just below the nostrils.

He opened his eyes and fell back a step. "That wasn't a kiss! What was *that*?"

"That's what kids who have been bad get instead of baby Jesus presents. A tickle under the nose with an armadillo tail."

He looked in her hand at something that could pass for the tip of some kind of animal tail—maybe a rat or gerbil if not an armadillo. He had never seen one of those up close. "I haven't been bad this year. I've been good!"

"I know—I was just teasing you."

"How about some presents, then? I know one I am dying to unwrap." He looked straight into her eyes and arched his eyebrows twice in a knowing way.

"First we have to give PawPaw Noel a Reveillon dinner and send him on his way."

PawPaw Noel said, "Ho, ho, ho, and a bottle of rum. No…wait…that's the pirate ditty. I mean, yeah, let's eat! I'm starving!"

"I hope you enjoy it, guys. I've been working on it all day—lobster, oysters, and shrimp. And then for dessert we're having a bûche de Noël!"

PawPaw Noel leaned into Brad and whispered, "That's yule log cake. Yummy!"

After dinner, throughout which PawPaw Noel remained in character and warned them of the dire consequences to little children of disobeying the Noel code throughout the year (such as being given a bottle of bayou water and a mud cake rather than an RC Cola and moon pie for Christmas lunch), the man announced it was finally time for presents.

"Le chat first."

Mary Lou explained, "Unless one of the humans finds the baby Jesus figurine baked into the bûche de Noël—and none of you guys did—the first presents go to the family pets. Just the indoor ones, not farm animals. And there is a distinct order of precedence. Dogs first, then cats, then raccoons, then lizards and snakes, next fish, and then last any pet beetles, lady bugs, gulf fritillaries, or other insects."

"What's that last one?"

"A gorgeous butterfly with yellow wings with black spots. They really brighten up any home."

"Oh, you mean a *monarch* butterfly?"

"No, those have black stripes on the wings, not spots. I mean a gulf fritillary. They're much prettier."

Brad shrugged. He was a biologist, after all, but had never spent much time on butterflies. Regarding insect studies, he had always focused on arthropod-borne diseases like malaria, typhus, and dengue, things with military significance.

"So anyway. You only have one pet—TomTom. So the cat goes first."

Brad shrugged again. "I didn't get him anything. Nothing for you guys either. I didn't know we were going to celebrate Christmas in February."

"It doesn't have to be an object. You can just spend extra time with him today, scratching him all over his cutesy little orange head with that big M pattern in front."

Hmm. Now I know what I can give Mary Lou for a present, too!

"I got TomTom some of those savory treats he likes."

"I got him a Fancy Feast," added PawPaw Noel.

"Oh, he loves those. Tombo!" Brad yelled toward the back room. "Fancy feast! Come and get it!"

The orange tabby came darting in, and PawPaw Noel opened the can and dumped the contents on the tiled floor with a loud wet *splatt*.

"We do have plates and bowls." Brad sniffed.

"Shuush!" whispered Mary Lou. "Don't you want your RC Cola and moon pie for next Christmas?"

10

Brad sat at the kitchen table, sipping green tea and watching Mary Lou putter about making shrimp jambalaya for dinner and musing over her distance ever since her father arrived and stayed in their house. She seemed especially concerned about keeping anything and everything very quiet in the bedroom. He was growing increasingly frustrated.

The phone rang, and she answered. Her face brightened, and she blurted out to no one in particular, "It's Ma!"

Sitting four or five feet away, Brad could hear the voice on the other end of the line nearly as well as Mary Lou's. It was a bellowing foghorn of a voice, with rapid-fire speech but very precise enunciation of each initial consonant, total loss of most final consonants, and heaven help the vowels. They just dragged out as if they were separate words, making Brad mentally want to clip them with scissors and cut them short.

"Ma, are you here? At the Baltimore train station?"

"Mais non, Cherie! I had a dreeem that the train would crash, so I got off in Gastonia and changed to a bus!"

"A bus? We sent you a free ticket for the train, and you wasted it?"

"Cherie-ee, cherie-ee, if I got keeled in a train crash, would that not waaste the ticket alzo? Non?"

"Never mind. When and where will your bus arrive?"

"I can tell you, but it will make no dee-ference, for I weel not bezon it!"

"Now what?"

"I had anuther dreem and got off in Reeesh-mon."

"Why on earth would you do a crazy thing like that?"

"Your father appeered to me in ze dreem as a bayou ghost and warned that a Rougarou had taken his place in your house! You must fleee, cherie. The man you have there is not your father. It eees a Rougarou!"

Brad looked up with a quizzical expression and silently mouthed the word *Rougarou.*

She covered the phone mouthpiece with one hand and whispered, "Cajun folklore. Some kind of boogey-man parents talk about to make their keeeds—I mean kids—behave."

Mary Lou looked exasperated. "Daddy?" she yelled at the top of her voice. "Ma is on the phone, and she is really up to it this time."

From the phone Brad heard, "I do not weesh to speek to that Rougarou!"

Dad came bounding in with a silly grin on his face and took the phone. Mary Lou sat next to Brad at the table. "Ho, beb, dôn be so coo-yôn! You scarin' you new son-in-law, and he be an outlaw! A real killer! You no wanna do some peeshwank thing like dat!"

"Ah not talk wit no Rougarou! Begone back to de bay-ous where youse belong!"

Mary Lou grabbed the phone back. "Ma! Enough of this nonsense! Daddy is right—Brad is an outlaw, and no Rougarou would dare hang around here. You'll be perfectly safe!"

"An outlaw, you say? You give me *freesôns* all over. Mebbe I come up for de wedding aftah all."

"Good. That's better."

"Ah said mebbe. Let me dreeem on it and see what your father tell me in my sleeep. Then ah deecide."

Mary Lou sighed. "Okay, Ma, you let us know what you dee-cide. I mean decide."

"Jus in caase, you better mebbe put in a good supply of garlic."

"Yes, Ma," she said with resignation.

"Rougarou no lak dat smell."

Mary Lou sighed. "I know, Ma."

"An' tell that Rougarou there be no messin' while I be there. I save myself for my reel husban'."

Brad looked at Dad in time to see his grin turn to a frown.

"Choooh!" he exclaimed.

"Ma, you know perfectly well there is no such thing as a Rougarou!"

"Ees there no such thang as elephant? Kangaroo? I see pictures of all of them at de Audubon Zoo in N'awleens. Right next de Rougarou statue."

Mary Lou's eyes flew wide. "That's just an exhibit with a manikin explaining the Cajun concept of the bayou Rougarou. It's still just a myth!"

"A meeth?"

"Yes, Ma, and you better be here in time for the wedding. Or I'll never let you be here for the birth."

"Don' be *boude*, Cherie. You wan' Ma at de weddin', ask Pa to tell me in my dreem dis nite. D'accord?"

"Sure, Ma, anything you say." She turned to Brad and mouthed silently, "Just like always."

"Honey chile, one more thang."

"Yeah, Ma?"

"When I left God's country for you weddeeen', Crazy Joe and Billy Bupp, dey tried to come wit me."

"Uh oh!"

Brad came to an abrupt attention. *Uh oh?*

"I tole dem dey couldna come."

"And?"

"And you know dey nevah lissen ta mee."

"Mon Dieu!" exclaimed Mary Lou.

"Sacré bleu!" added Dad. "How many guns yoo got in dis house?"

Mary Lou hung up the phone, and Dad trudged out of the room with his head hung low, muttering something about how if he were the porcupine king that Josephine must be the skunk queen. The last thing Brad could hear before the man got too far away was, "Poor Pee-aire. He not gonna get lucky dis trip. Sacré bleu!"

Brad shared his dismay. *Looks like no one is getting any in this house until after the wedding.* He leaned over and whispered to Mary Lou, "Please tell me you were adopted. Right?"

The new code on eBay that people are using to buy and sell radioactive materials. Am I interpreting correctly, or is this a projection of my own imagination?

Brad sat at his desk in his home office, which doubled as his eBay war room. Peering at the bright computer screen and sipping on Celestial Seasons Blueberry Breeze green tea, he pondered.

He had noted for years now that when eBay changed its rules or tried to enforce its standard rules more strictly, that customers who didn't like that tried to find ways to thwart the system. For instance, while it was against the rules to sell alcohol as such, people could get away with it on eBay by selling small, miniature, or collectible bottles which just happened to contain liquor. In other words, technically they weren't selling liquor but were rather selling classic, sealed bottles, which just by pure coincidence happened to contain alcohol.

Then when eBay moved to forbid Nazi items, a huge horde of World War II sellers and collectors were completely dismayed. Dealers began to move their items to other categories. For instance, those with Nazi stamps—most bearing the image of Adolf himself, and you couldn't get more Nazi than that—started advertising in the stamp category rather than the military category. For Nazi paper currency bearing the swastika emblem, they moved to the currency category.

Those with gear such as Nazi military caps with swastika insignia, where there really wasn't another appropriate category, began to describe their items more subtly. Then in the item picture, they would discreetly cover up the swastika or angle the camera so that it didn't show.

After the radium paint episode, with its lethally strong amount of radioactive material that AFRRI had tracked and reported to the FBI, eBay wisely forbade the buying and selling of dangerous amounts of radioactive material, but they still allowed the open trade in safe amounts of radioactive elements such as uranium, radium, and thorium, or collector's items that had been made radioactive as a novelty or keepsake, such as the low-level radioactive marbles, AFRRI itself produced by exposing them to its pulsing nuclear reactor and offered as free souvenirs to VIP visitors.

So what option did that leave to those who wanted to sell verboten amounts of highly radioactive material? As part of his military mission at AFRRI, Brad continued to scour eBay for the sale of radioactive materials and information materials such as military technical reports, manuals, and handbooks providing knowledge on nuclear weapons. eBay proved very cautious and careful in forbidding classified materials, so that info area had never in Brad's experience sent up red flags. People were buying and selling things you could acquire in a library or openly online or via the Freedom of Information Act.

But that left one category that still concerned Brad. There seemed to be a handful of dealers describing their sales of radioactive source material in a code that would bypass eBay censors and only be understood by professional experts or those otherwise in the know. For the moment, Brad was calling it a *phonetic code.*

For instance, the auction he had been tracking in the science and radiation section for several days now and had just reported to Colonel Fukioki at AFRRI was for "esselon dust." You could buy it by the ounce for as many ounces as you wanted to well past the safety cut off into highly dangerous rad territory. As a radiation expert, Brad knew there was no such thing…or rather, there never had been such a thing by that name related to radiation. The first time he saw it he kept repeating it to himself, trying to discern the meaning.

"Esselon? Esselun? Esselone? Ess-ell-one? SL-1? The 1961 stationary low-power reactor number one?"

When he spelled it like that, he immediately remembered the tragedy of how a momentary screw-up with a single control rod led to an explosion, which completely destroyed the nuclear reactor, killed its three operators, exposed eight hundred rescue and clean-up workers to potentially dangerous levels of radiation, and led to literally tons of highly radioactively contaminated material. It seemed totally inconceivable to Brad, but for nearly forty years, enough material to kill thousands of people lay in a shallow grave in an open field protected by nothing but an ordinary fence and some signs warning passersby to keep away from the dangerous radioactive zone.

Had someone really sneaked in there and, at great risk to themselves, slipped a few buckets of material out? If not, what on earth else could esselon be?

And the other auction Brad had been tracking really made his hair stand up. Was he interpreting the code on that one correctly? Did someone actually locate the radio-active hand of death? And were they really trying to sell it on eBay? Something that could deliver a killing dose to anyone who handled it unprotected for fifteen minutes or less?

And why were the many bidders on that item so eager to get it?

12

Brad got home from work to find Dad, the remains of a scowl on his face, sitting in Brad's own favorite chair by the front window, reading a copy of the New Orleans *Times-Picayune*. It was the same copy of the newspaper that he had picked up at the Lafayette airport the day he began his journey up north. Brad had noted him reading it every single day since. Either the man was a slow reader, or he enjoyed some taste of Louisiana, even if it was the same taste over and over again. But how interesting could it be on the fourth or fifth reading?

"Say, Dad, where's Mary Lou? I noticed her car was gone."

"She lef' in big huff. Tired of me bein' in her way or sompin' like dat."

"Did you guys have an argument?"

"No such thing in a Cajun household. Daddy lay down de law. Daddy say what is. Kids take it or go. Dey don' argue."

"And?"

"Kid go."

"No, I see that. What did you lay down the law about?"

"Where you gone live aftah da weddin'. Where raise kids."

"And, might I ask, where did you tell her?"

"Down by de bayou, course. Cajun grandkids gotta grow up in Cajun country like every other generation since we expelled from Acadia by those British arses in the middle seventeen hundreds."

Brad crossed his arms across his chest. "Dad?"

"Yes?"

"There's just one flaw in your argument."

"What dat?"

"You said Daddy knows best in a Cajun household, right?"

"There the truth! But Mary Lou not lak it."

"But, Dad, *I'm* the daddy in this household. I lay down the law."

"You no Cajun!"

"The heck I'm not! Maybe not by birth, but Mary Lou adopted me as a Cajun long ago. She even appointed me a special Cajun nickname. You're the porcupine king, and I'm the owl master."

"That does be a good Cajun name. Very high honor, that one. Owl de wisest creature on de bayou."

"And I do consider that name a badge of honor…and the emblem of me being an adopted Cajun. So Mary Lou now looks to me to lay down the law, as you put it."

"Poor Pee-aire, he no can catch break. He like second tail on de ox."

"Dad, don't worry about it. You know the army tells me where to go. I don't really have a choice. You were in the guard."

"Never left Louisiane. In my day de guard always stay home."

"Yeah, but I know when you joined up, signed your papers, and swore the loyalty oath they explained they could send you anywhere in the world...whether you liked it or not."

"Dat true. Pee-aire, he wanta see world, but never catch a break."

"I tell you what, Dad, how about I fix you a drink? Want some more Maker's Mark?"

"Pee-aire finish dat bottle."

"I know. I just bought a new one at the class six."

The man's face brightened. "Thanks, son, I would like a drink. Neat. At least four fingers worth."

"Coming right up."

"I haven't been to a class six since I left the guard! That was the most magical place I ever went in all my born days. A million kinds of beer and whiskey an' cheaper than anywhere else. And no tax to the revenuers! Best part yet!"

Brad smiled. *How odd—a change in Dad's mood has led to a change in his speech pattern. What is going on here?*

"You reckon you could get me in to see yours? I think I'd adopt you as a Cajun, too, if you could do that." The man grinned his biggest since that first minute at the airport, revealing perfect Hollywood teeth. No backwoods primitive type.

"Sure, Dad, we can go this coming Saturday if you want."

"Oh, yeah! Pee-aire want!"

"Just make sure to let me handle the goods and pay for them. I'll have to show my military ID to do that. They won't let you haul stuff to the counter and buy it."

"Dat swell. Pee-aire love when sommin else buy."

His speech is changing back again. What the heck is this all about? Brad returned with the whiskey and a huge mug of de-caf green tea for himself.

"Here, Dad. Listen, while we have a few minutes alone, why don't you tell me about yourself, how you grew up, met Ma, and so on. Mary Lou hasn't told me much about you guys yet."

Dad took a long pull off the straight whiskey and sighed. "Thanks, son, that is good stuff. So what do you wanna know?"

"Whatever you consider important about your background. Anything that might help me understand Mary Lou better. You know, stuff like that."

"Well, I may be Cajun, but actually I was a city boy, born and raised in Lafayette. That's only a few miles from the bayous, but it's still a city. So I was never really much of a swamp rat growing up."

"But did you never leave the city?"

"Oh, sure, every year we went to the Breaux Bridge Crawfish Festival not far out of town. And on weekends we'd go boatin' on the Vermilion River or fishing or campin' when the weather was right and there weren't too many mosquitoes.

"Even in the city we had some cool Cajun stuff like the Acadian Village Park with a replica village from the old Cajun days, including some original buildings. Cyprus

Lake, right there on the university campus, with alligators and everything. And the Cajun Heartland State Fair every year, right there on the Cajundome grounds."

"Dad, let me interrupt for a second."

"Yeah?"

"Do you realize you have lapsed out of speaking Cajun and are now sticking mostly to standard English?"

"You caught that, did you? I got so involved thinking about my childhood that I forgot to keep it up."

"So it's an act with you? At least partly?"

The older man looked up toward the ceiling. "You could say that. I told you I was a city boy. My father was a professor at the University of Southwestern Louisiana—that's what they called it in those days. He was in the math department. Brilliant man. So I grew up with one leg in an educated, refined home."

"And the other?"

"Amidst a bunch of Cajuns who thought that was only sissy stuff. Traitorous, really. You could get beat up if you put on airs. They looked at it like you were betraying your birthright or heritage or something."

Brad mused, thinking back to his own childhood when bullies picked on him for one reason or another, usually because he seemed too smart or got good grades. "Wow, Dad, that's painful being torn in two like that."

"Son, I have a confession to make."

"Yeah, Dad?"

"I did it with you, too. That was my Cajun leg talking when I told you my pa named me after Pierre Lafitte, Jean's older brother."

"Well, you fooled me with that one. It rang true to me, what with all your pirate and blood lust talk."

"My pa really named me after the famous French mathematician of the seventeenth century, Pierre de Fermat, one of the founders of number theory and probability, of analytic geometry and elementary calculus."

"Whew! I'll bet your educated leg got kicked pretty hard when the kids caught wind of that."

"Specially after they just flunked a math test."

"So it's a role you play to blend in. And you're the brains of the family. I knew Mary Lou was brilliant, finishing top in the state in accounting, but I was beginning to wonder if she were adopted."

Dad laughed then leaned forward and lowered his voice. "Let me tell you something man to man, son."

"Sure."

"Don't tell Mary Lou I told you this."

"Okay."

"Whenever I'm around Ma or even just talking to her on the phone, like the other night, I put my Cajun disguise on PDQ! And it stays on for a long, long time."

"I see."

"Mary Lou does it a little bit, too. You noticed her on the phone starting to talk like Ma?"

"Of course."

"Here's the man to man part."

"Okay…" *Just spill it already!*

"When Ma gets here, I strongly advise you to do the same."

"Really? What happens if I don't?"

Dad pulled back a scruffy patch of thick hair that had lain across the right forehead and pointed. "See this scar?"

Brad nodded.

Dad pointed to two short but livid scars on his left forearm. "See these?"

Brad nodded again.

"Nuff said."

"Nawww, you're not getting off that easy. What happened to your forehead?"

"Well, I wanted Mary Lou to grow up with two legs also. Ma was teaching her everything about being Cajun and speaking Cajun and all that, but on the sly, when Ma wasn't around, I was teaching that sweet little thing how to speak regular English, too, just in case she ever wanted or needed to fit into the outside world. If I hadn't done that, she never would have come up here and met you. You two would never be tying the reins together. And you two wouldn't be making the bestest pair of Cajun twins any of us is likely to see in this lifetime."

"I'm grateful to you, Dad. I mean that. Mary Lou means more to me than any girl I've ever met or dreamed about."

"Ah, yes, dreamed about. Your dreams can stand in the way of real happiness, can't they? You dream of the big two hundred pound catfish that will make you *the* fisherman of all time and then you can't enjoy just regular cat fishing for Sunday dinner."

"You're a very wise man, Dad. The complete opposite of the man who spawned me but never taught me a good and decent thing in all his miserable days."

"Mary Lou told me something about your background. I know it's tough to overcome something like that, and I'm proud of you for doing it."

Brad felt uncomfortable thinking back to those terrible days with Pop. "So you still haven't told me how you got that scar."

"Oh, I was hoping to distract you from that. It ain't a pretty story. Not the kind of thing a Cajun man would like to admit."

"Spill it, Dad."

"Okay, then. One day Ma came home and caught me giving proper speech lessons to our little girl. She blew up like a tank of swamp gas tetched by lightning. I don't think she really meant to hurt me, but she just started throwing a fit and then throwing things, and an old RC Cola bottle whupped me up the side of my head, broke, and cut me pretty good."

"Wow! I don't think I ever want to get on Ma's bad side."

"Best you don't."

"So how about the forearm?"

"I gave you one. But I ain't telling you the story of t'other one till after you two are properly married."

"Why?"

"Cause I don't want to get kilt for scaring you off of joining this family!"

"Oh, Dad, don't be so melodramatic. I'm a grown up. I think I can handle it.

"No dice. Not this day." The man looked determined.

Brad shrugged. "Okay, then, tell me more about Ma's life and background."

"She never left St. Martin Parish in all her life…until this week."

"So you basically speak Cajun as a second language, just as I, after studying it in college for three years, can start spouting German when I need to and just turn it off when I don't. You're more like half Cajun. But she's the real thing, through and through."

"Two hundred percent Cajun, that one."

"Dad, your father was a mathematician."

"I know, I know. There can't be more than one hundred percent of a single item. I took math at USL, too. Got all As. Think of me what you like, son, but understand when I lapse into Cajun around Ma that I am fond of survival and good times and sweet lovin'. A Cajun's gotta do what a Cajun's gotta do."

"I understand, Dad. I did pretty much the same thing when I was first courting your daughter. I immersed myself in Cajun food, music, football—anything and everything to get closer to her."

"Then you understand what I mean by the lure of the Cajun woman. No place else on God's green earth produces women like that."

"I do. They're just more natural and…and…*real*, I guess, and earthy, at least judging by Mary Lou. She's actually the only one I've ever met."

"Wait'll you meet Ma. Then you'll see the source of that special elixir, that bayou magic. I tell you, son, it sings to me day and night. I'll never get that magic song out of my head, my heart. Never want to, neither. Oh, Brad, wait till you see her! She's still the most beautiful and shapely woman in that whole parish!"

"So Mary Lou got your brains but her looks."

The older man nodded, smiling. "Oh, yeah…oh, yeah."

"So if you really came from two different worlds, how did you two meet? Fall in love? Get married? Were you in school together or something?"

"No, we came from two different parishes. Nearby but different. Lafayette for me, next door St. Martin for her. One day when I was about sixteen, my father took all of us to St. Martinville to see the Evangeline statue and exhibit and all that other stuff on Acadiana. Josephine was a volunteer tour guide at the Acadian Memorial Museum. One look at her, and I didn't see anything else at the museum that whole day. I just kept following her around, joining one group after the next until she drew me aside and told me in no uncertain terms to get lost."

Brad laughed. "This is a cool story, Dad. I love it! What happened next?"

"What would you do? I grabbed her and kissed her right there in front of everybody in the whole museum!"

"And?"

"I think she was about to slap me, but everyone around us started clapping and cheering. Then she musta realized what I already knew…that we made the perfect couple.

"After that I borrowed my father's car every weekend I could and drove over to her place to court her proper-like. Her father didn't cotton to me much at first. He didn't think I was Cajun enough. But her mother brought

PawPaw around by teaching me how to swing low through the bayou, wrestle gators, hunt, trap, and fish. Tan hides— you name it."

"So you had to prove your bona fides to wed a Cajun lass."

"Hupp! There's one right there, son. No one down the bayou say lass. You say fille for daughter, pischouette for a mischievous little girl, copine for a friend who is female, or gaienne for girlfriend. Capisce?"

Brad laughed out loud. "Now you're throwing in Italian words. Don't think you fooled me with that one. So once you proved your Cajun-hood, then what?"

"We got married two years later, right after I finished high school and joined the guard. And a couple of years later I started attending USL on the GI bill."

Just then Mary Lou walked in the front door with a bag of groceries. She smiled at Brad then looked over her shoulder at Dad in the easy chair and just sniffed at him.

She waddled into the kitchen without a word with Brad close behind. A thought struck him, and he paused in the doorway and turned back to Dad. "You learned how to fight in the guard, right?

"Are you kidding? I even boxed for a while. And I earned my third stripe because I was the best hand-to-hand combat instructor in the unit."

"And you can pull that, pardon the expression, Cajun coonass routine any time you want, right?"

"Mais oui, mahn!"

"How would you like to help me take down the rest of that terrorist group that tried to kill Mary Lou and the twins a couple of months ago?"

A warrior's visage crossed Dad's face, and his arms stiffened. He shook his head. "I'll make 'em wish they were up to their necks in alligators instead."

"Good…I've got an idea."

The phone rang in the kitchen, and Brad picked it up. "Hello?"

No answer. No sound.

"I said *hello!*"

Still nothing. "If someone is there, I can't hear you. There must be a bad connection. Please hang up and dial again."

"You no soun' lak Rougarou." It was a big foghorn of a voice.

"No, I'm not."

"You muss be Brad. C'est vrais?"

"Ma, nice to talk to you. Are you in Baltimore yet?"

"Mais non!"

"Still in Richmond?"

"Bah! Non! Reesh-mon full of sheets. Nuttin' but sheets."

"Where are you then?"

"Ah no can tell you."

"Why not? You can trust me. Remember, A'm, I mean, I'm an outlaw."

"Ah do nah know where I am. It look like cabin back home, but this cahn't be God's countree."

Brad rolled his eyes and lowered the phone. "Mary Lou! Your mother is on the phone!" he yelled.

"Sweet rattlesnake claws, boy! Don't yell ta girl lak dat. You done scare de bebs for sure."

"Coming!" yelled Mary Lou.

Brad grimaced. If his yelling voice was no louder than Ma's regular speaking voice, how could he scare the unborn babies but she would not? "Sorry."

"Chooo! Lissen, boy. You gotta talk nice to dem bebs. Ever night and ever morning, you rub cherie's big belly wit yo hand and talk sweet and low at her belly. Sing douce Cajun songs like "Bayou Baby." Let dem bebs know daddy good man. Dere world be good place. No fear for Cajun bebs comin' inta da world. C'est vrais?"

That actually makes some sense. I'm going to try that. Never did learn a thing about good parenting from Pop. His only claim to virtue was that he worked hard and provided for us. But everything else was fists and rage. "Sure, Ma, anything you say." Brad had a feeling he would be saying that a lot in the next few days. Probably in the next few years.

Beaming, Mary Lou waddled into the room and took the phone. "Ma, are you in Richmond still or in Baltimore?"

"Reesh-mon full of sheets. Ever-where nuttin' but sheets."

"Ma, what on earth do you mean? What happened? Where are you?"

"One t'ing atta time, cherie. My brain 'bout to explode when you shoot so much at once."

"Sorry, Ma. Did you have trouble in Richmond?"

"Nuttin' but trouble down there. Ever'body coo-yôn rite there. If not coo-yôn, dey motier foux! De rest be bon rien. What a potain down there in Reesh-mon!"

Mary Lou covered the phone with one hand and whispered a translation to Brad. "Everyone down there is stupid, half crazy, good for nothing, or all three. What a ruckus!"

Brad nodded.

"Do you want us to come get you, Ma?"

"Non, cherie. In my dreem las' nite you pere return' and tol' me to stay here one more day, mebbe more. Much trouble up your way. Danger!"

"Oo ye yi! Ma, not that Rougarou business again. We're all gettin'—I mean getting—tired of that."

"Non, cherie. Pa tol' in my dreem that your Rougarou is good Rougarou, sen' ta protect you an' dey bebs."

"A good Rougarou?"

"Oui, ma fille. Once a year when the alligators dance, the Rougarou, he can only attack de ee-vil, not the good peoples. That Rougarou in yo hous' will help Brad stop de ee-vil jess befoh da wed-deen. Pa tol' me in dah dreem. You will see."

Mary Lou frowned. "Ma, gar ici! You better get up here in time for da—the—wedding! Or else!"

"It all work out in da en'. Yoo see. Pa tol' me. Jess when you all alone 'n all is dark, Brad and de Rougarou who has Pa's shape will save you an' dee bebs. And you Ma come up da wed-deen an' hol' you hand. Doo-na worry, ma honey-chile. Ah bee dere when da time rite."

"Ma, where the heck are you, anyway?"

"I do-nah know. Gotta hang up de phones now, beb. See de po-leece comin' again. Au revoir, beb." She hung up.

Mary Lou looked very cross but didn't move or say anything for a long moment. Stiffly, she hung up the phone, turned to Brad, placed both hands on her hips, and said, "Something tells me you know exactly what Ma is talking about."

"Don't look at me! I've never even met the woman. I only talked to her for half a minute."

"Okay, then where is Dad?"

"He's running an errand for me. He'll be gone for a long, long time."

"Brad—I'm waiting for an explanation!"

"I'm not going to tell you till we've made love…twice!"

14

Brad got his first peek at the goods as he chased Mary Lou around the kitchen, clawing at her blouse as they darted around the table.

At least she tried to dart. With her baby bump having grown noticeably over recent weeks, she soon tired of the exercise and backed into the fridge, panting, her chest heaving as her sparkling eyes met his.

He quickly moved in to grab her, and she put up her hands in front and made a mock squeal of protest that made him want her even more. It had been days…too many days…and they both needed this.

He held her tight, gave her a quick kiss, then finished unbuttoning her blouse.

She looked up slyly. "Are you sure Daddy's gone? Far away? For a long, long time?"

He nodded, his whole body aflame with desire.

"Then come and get it. And I don't mean dinner."

After enjoying each other—twice as promised—Brad rolled over on his side with his left ear on her belly, looking up at her face. She had her right arm curled behind her head to prop it up and looked stunningly gorgeous. The most beautiful woman alive, he thought.

"What did Ma mean on the phone about when the alligators dance?" At the time it had given Brad the image of the alligators dancing on their hind legs with the hippos in Disney's animated *Fantasia*. But he knew that couldn't be what Ma meant.

"That's what they call the mating display for alligators. While the female watches, the big bull gator bellows and roars and puts on a show in the water. The underwater sounds they make vibrate so strongly that the water splashes and sparkles above the surface—almost like some kind of fountain—even when the body isn't visibly moving. It is a sight to behold! If she is impressed enough, the female swims over and says, in her own way, "Let's do this thing." He rubs snouts with her and then follows her to a brushy patch near the water where they can get it on."

"Yeah, but this is still winter. Mating season's gotta be in spring, right?"

"Well, if Ma says now is the time of the alligator dance, then I guess the gators will just have to push their schedule up a bit to please her."

"What on earth?"

"Brad, there's one thing you've got to realize if you're going to get along with this family. Ma is a force of nature all unto herself. The phrase all of us learned early on is—"

"Whatever you say, Ma. Yeah, I know. She's got me saying it already."

She smiled. "Good. Looks like I'm marrying a wise owl master."

What a crazy family I'm marrying into. "Sing "Bayou Baby" for me."

"That's a Cajun lullaby. How did you hear about that?"

"Ma mentioned it over the phone, but I want to hear it with the music and everything."

"Okay."

In her soft, melodic voice, she sang, and Brad felt transported to another world. He felt relaxed, trouble free, and loved, just plain loved. *What an incredible, captivating tune!*

He propped himself up on his left elbow right beside her, and began to softly rub her belly with gentle, circular motions. Then he looked straight at her belly button as he rubbed above it. "Hey, Remy and Cindy Lou, this is Daddy. I'm looking forward to seeing you soon. Your mom and I love you already. Mamere and Papere, too."

Then he sang softly, almost in a whisper, the few lines of the lullaby he could remember from his only hearing so far.

> I'll fly o'er that bayou to you
> Oh bayou, my baby on the bayou tonight
> We'll dream of tomorrow,
> when the fishin' is through
> I'll fly o'er that bayou to you.

Softly, ever so softly, he kissed her sweet tummy. "Night night, kids. See you soon!"

Then he looked up and smiled at her—his woman, mother of his children, partner for life.

She was crying.

Sitting at his desk, staring at the computer screen at what he believed was a coded auction on eBay for the radioactive hand of death, Brad mused how true radiation exposure accidents were usually triggered by careless experts who knew better but did something stupid and lost radioactive materials, followed up by hapless individuals who had no clue what they were handling when they found and retrieved them.

Then there were the deliberate incidents where rad experts knew exactly what they handled and then did it intentionally anyway, either to commit suicide or homicide.

For instance, in Moscow on June 8, 1960, a rad worker who was only nineteen but clearly wanted to die stole a powerful cesium-137 source. He sneaked a vial of the material from his own lab, put it in his left pants pocket for several hours, and then to make sure, shifted it to various positions on his body for a total of about twenty hours exposure. It was estimated that he absorbed between fifteen hundred and two thousand rads to his body as a whole, easily four to six times a lethal dose. In fact, symptoms appeared within just hours, though he lingered for fifteen days before expiring.

In Bulgaria in 1972, there was a similar suicide by a worker with radioactive materials, an expert whose career was using radiation to test for defects in various items of equipment. He had a known history of early family trauma but appeared only mildly bipolar—alternating between mild depression and excited or hypomanic states—but was able to function in society. But when he decided he had had enough of the world, over a period of a couple of hours, he deliberately exposed his heart and other body areas to cesium-137. This led to extremely high localized doses and subsequent injury, but it took him four months of suffering to die. He was only thirty years old.

In Tulsa, Oklahoma, on July 29, 1981, an industrial radiographer who had lost his job killed himself by exposing his own flesh to the kind of iridium-192 source he had frequently used in his former job. Sort of a poetic justice in a way, though directed at himself.

Then there were those who committed homicide with radioactive materials—not more or less random terrorists attacking a place such as an airport or football game, injuring and killing whoever happened to be there, but rather a deliberate homicide directed at a specific individual but using radiation rather than a gun or knife to do the deed. For instance, in Moscow on April 14, 1993, one or more employees of the Kartontara packing company decided to take out their boss Vladimir Kaplun. They stuck a small amount of radioactive material under his chair, where it slowly cooked him from the buttocks up into his torso and down into his legs over the hours each day he sat in his chair. It was a weak enough dose where it took some time for symptoms to appear, but by then the outcome was sure. It took him a month in the hospital to die.

Then there were the dirty bomb incidents where the bomb was never detonated but rather reported to the police, apparently in an effort to spread alarm and terror without actually hurting anyone and possibly bringing down the swift wrath of the populace and law enforcement. For instance, at the Izmaylovsky Park in Moscow in November, 1995, a Chechen separatist group prepared and deposited a dirty bomb, which included explosives and radioactive cesium-137. But instead of exploding it, they alerted the media to its position, and it was safely removed.

And then there were the incidents still in the making that Brad was trying to track down on eBay. He read again the listing in the science and radiation section, which most concerned him at the moment.

> Esselon dust. Lots of esselon dust. Then there are the occasional large chunks. I wish someone could give me a hand with these. So many auctions to complete and so little time! Sure could use a hand. This chunk weighs about two pounds, maybe a hair more or less. I'm selling the dust by the ounce in my other auctions, so please check those out. But this is for a single chunk weighing about two pounds. Great for science experiments and stuff.

This was not the pure phonetic code which Brad had first figured out where esselon stood, he believed, for ess-el-one or SL-1. This auction used what Brad considered a hybrid code. First it tipped off people in the know, scientists or others knowledgeable about radioactive matters, by referring to the SL-1 incident phonetically. But then it used hint words or euphemisms to refer to what Brad concluded was the SL-1's radioactive hand of death. The word *hand* was mentioned twice in two sentences, which didn't really make sense for an eBay auction, on the surface referring to the seller's personal issues, which were irrelevant to buyers. Clue number three was that this was not dust but rather a single piece, one weighing in the range of an adult male hand. Of course, in the SL-1 remains burial ground there was no doubt a huge variety in the size and weight of the thousands of pieces of radioactive debris. But clue number four referred to hair, which if meant literally, would make this a fleshly rather than metallic item.

Brad realized he could be off base, but what if he was right? If he was incorrect, what else could this item description possibly be referring to? If he had the SL-1 part right, no other item in the debris field from the neutron criticality explosion would be that weight and have hair.

But there was another twist to this eerie mystery. Would the human hand that was converted to an intense emitter of radiation by the massive infusion of neutrons in that awful instant where the hand poised over the reactor's open mouth—the control rod's hole—still be intact forty-one years later? Or would it have rotted?

Brad really had nothing precise to go on here. Never before and never since in the annals of nuclear science had human flesh itself not merely sustained damage but turned into a dangerously potent radioactive source. So there was absolutely nothing he knew of in the scientific literature to answer that question. Based on general biological principles, he guessed that it was possible it would survive as an intact hand. After all, ordinary flesh buried in the soil quickly decayed through the dual action of microorganisms breaking open and feeding on the cells and larger organisms such as worms plowing right through and eating it.

But the radiation in this hand of death could deliver a killing dose to a full-grown man in just a few minutes, so it would certainly destroy any attacking bacteria or worms. The hand might be essentially mummified but still largely with its appearance intact—at least as of the awful final moment of the explosion. It must have looked blasted and burned but still recognizably human when the rescuers darted out of the reactor building with the body intact that first day.

In case the brood was behind either the selling or buying of this item, Brad did not want to use his own eBay handle to bid on this. They would recognize that from his last encounter with them. He asked Dad to do so instead.

Mary Lou's father had never used eBay before, but Brad walked him through the process and registered him with the handle Cajun-Dad. Then to provide cover, he used Dad's account to bid on several different scientific items so as not to seem too preoccupied with this one. Items such as a micrometer, test tubes, and a Bunsen burner. Then he plunked down a bid for an even seventy-five dollars on the radioactive hand, the mark of a novice or someone who wasn't particularly competitive or scheming, as Brad himself was.

Immediately, the high bid rose to seventy-six dollars, as the current high bidder apparently had chosen the automatic bid option.

Now to look at the other bidders. So far only three.

The low bidder so far was ScienceGuyNotNye. Brad checked his other auctions. Reagant bottles, graduated bottles, a box of safety goggles, test tubes, uranium test sources, a radiac meter, laboratory jacks, tripods, tongs, and pH test papers. Pretty much standard science lab type stuff in Brad's opinion. Nothing to suggest a malevolent plan. This guy looked like a high school general science teacher restocking his school supplies. Or maybe an amateur home scientist.

The next higher bidder was BlueSkyMontana. Brad first checked to see if he had selling auctions open, and he did. Brad wanted to know if he really hailed from Montana, and each of the selling auctions claimed exactly that. Brad then checked that eBayer's bidding auctions. A little more suspicious pattern here. He had bids on esselon dust, the hand (or chunk) auction, and a Geiger counter. Could be a scientist with an interest in radiation, but this pattern could also fit someone with a more malicious intent.

Next up was Dad's bid, and then the person who had so far held the lead for some days now—MealyMouth. What an odd handle, Brad thought. In his last adventure he had run across people with ominous sounding handles, which rather accurately portrayed them or those that portrayed a glamorous self-image, though usually inaccurately. Some eBay nicknames just pointed to some key interest or concern of their own, such as ChemGuy or Brad's own TomTom_III, named after the family cat.

MealyMouth just didn't seem like anything a normal person would pick for himself or herself. Mealy? Mouth? MealyMouth? What did that expression really mean, anyway? To Brad it had always just seemed like an inexplicable term of derision, like craphead. Not something you could take literally. Meal in the mouth? Mouth full of meal? He decided to look it up in the dictionary.

Aha! Mealy Mouthed was defined in the online Free Dictionary as "Unwilling to state facts or opinions simply and directly." It came from an old German term referring to someone with a mouth so full of meal that he couldn't speak plainly. But Brad could see a whole new significance now. It didn't mean the person mumbled his words, as in the expression mush-mouth today. Rather it meant someone who refused to speak plainly, to tell the truth. Someone being evasive—a con man, if you will.

Why, all these coded radiation auctions were mealy-mouthed in that sense. This guy is proclaiming he's a member of this inside group! Almost paradoxical, for these guys are being evasive, and MealyMouth is honestly saying he is a member of this dishonest group!

That gave Brad a scary thought. What if these seemingly unrelated guys were actually affiliated in some way, perhaps loosely, and were using eBay not only to buy and sell but to communicate plans with each other? Say there was a brood in one part of the country that wanted to coordinate an attack or other plot with the remains of the Frederick area brood. Maybe in their auctions they are using code to communicate plans as well as items.

After all, with the new anti-terrorism laws such as the USA Patriot Act of 2001 in operation, suspects were far more likely these days to have someone monitoring their phone and e-mail activity. Did the NSA also monitor their eBay activity for terrorist plans? Maybe the brood had discovered the safest way to communicate was through eBay auctions. Through the eBay code!

What else does MealyMouth like on eBay? Brad checked his other auctions, including the ones already closed. *Hmm. Not clear cut, but suggestive. Could mean something.* This individual had already bought several ounces of esselon dust and now clearly wanted this hand or so-called chunk. In addition, he had bought a book on radiation shielding, one on radiation detection, and some lead sheeting, including some pure lead-barrel vise shims and a vise-grip.

What are shims for? Brad looked it up. *Hmm. Can be shaped and used to fill cracks, holes, and the like. This guy is building something with lead, and he wants to make sure it is one hundred percent sealed. That's just what I would do if I were going to carry the radioactive hand of death somewhere.*

But where? Where does he want to carry it, and what will he do with it when he gets there? Can I crack the rest of this eBay code before it is too late?

Brad sat with TomTom in his lap in the living room in his special chair reading Dad's old *Times Picayune*, trying to figure out what the older man found so special about it. As far as Brad could see, the only thing of interest to him personally was the article about the upcoming summit at Camp David. Living where he did, Brad was used to seeing the helicopters flying overhead on their way from the White House South Lawn helipad to Camp David now and then. Never the exact same route, but once in a while he'd see the marine choppers for the advance party, or one of the half dozen decoy VH-3D Sea Kings they used in the presidential "shell game," continually changing the flight formation to keep anyone from identifying by visual the president's actual ride, known by the call sign Marine One. With the constant aerial realignment, Brad had no way to know if the president actually rode inside whichever one he was looking at.

Odd to have a Camp David event announced so far in advance. When the president just came up for a weekend of R and R, they never announced that until afterward, just as a security precaution. But since this was one of the very rare and important summits intended to foster peace in the Middle East, they apparently wanted to give it maximum publicity. Brad hadn't noted it yet in his local paper, but here it was in a Louisiana one.

Very odd.

✗

"Mary Lou, have you gotten today's mail yet?"

"Sure did, sweetie. It's on the kitchen table."

"Anything from Victoria?"

"Nope."

"That's unusual. Usually she sends at least a card about every other day. I think it's been three or four days now with no word."

"Maybe she got too busy meeting an article deadline to write to you for a while. Or maybe she met someone and has been dating on the trip."

"That would be nice. She hasn't been out with anyone since Mark Perkins." The brood member sent to spy on them by befriending Mary Lou and insinuating himself into the family by dating Victoria.

"I wish she could find someone, Brad. Someone stable and nice like you, someone she can be happy with forever. I don't see how we three are going to make it much longer in the same house. Especially when the twins arrive. She'll have no patience with all the noise, the baby stuff in her way. All the spew and pooh."

"On the other hand, we'd have a built-in babysitter."

Mary Lou appeared in the doorway between the kitchen and living room. "You've got to be kidding me! She won't know how to take care of infant twins! No way that's going to happen."

Brad didn't want to add to the tension, so he said nothing and glumly looked back at the newspaper. TomTom licked Brad's hand as if to comfort him.

But Mary Lou continued. "By the way, exactly where is Dad? He's been gone an awfully long time. What kind of errand did you send him on, anyway?"

"He's looking for lead coffins."

"Lead *coffins*?"

April 13, 1970

Brad remembered being very moved by the realistic portrayals of character and danger in the 1995 film *Apollo 13* starring Tom Hanks and Ed Harris. A vivid, suspenseful film, it introduced two enduring phrases into the English language, both of which Brad often quoted.

The first was "Houston, we have a problem." That one merely became a cute way of announcing an approaching dilemma or ongoing difficulty.

The second, "Failure is not an option," said in the movie by Ed Harris, was one of Brad's favorite phrases and one of the mottoes by which he lived his life.

All but forgotten, Brad thought ruefully, was the fact that the real accident that threatened the lives of all aboard also led to a potentially catastrophic radiation accident on earth. Aboard the lunar module was a small nuclear power device, a radioisotope thermoelectric generator or RTG that contained about eight and half pounds of highly radioactive plutonium-238, enough to kill a large number of people if the device had landed at just the wrong location—say Grand Central Station in Chicago—and exploded in just the wrong way.

Instead, the module with the RTG still intact landed in the Pacific Ocean and settled somewhere south of Fiji into the Tonga Trench, one of the deepest spots in the ocean about five miles below the surface. Brad saw the NRC updates that reported the results of the periodic radiation scans ever since, and it appeared the external cladding protecting the rad source was still intact, and the RTG was not leaking radiation.

Brad knew the cladding would eventually deteriorate from exposure to salt water and start leaking…by one estimate in about eight hundred and seventy years. However, by that time the source material would have lost much of its radioactive punch. The half life of plutonium-238, the time period during which half of the initial radioactive material breaks down, is about eighty-eight years.

In class Brad once worked out the computation. If one started with the RTG's 44,500 curies of radioactive plutonium 238, in about eighty-eight years there would be only about twenty-two thousand left. Another eighty-eight years would leave only eleven thousand left. And so on. After ten half lives it would be down to only roughly one-one thousandth of the starting amount, not nearly as dangerous.

$$\times$$

September 30, 1988

Brad knew the Soviets were somewhat less lucky when their nuclear-powered satellite Cosmos 1900 lost communication with earth. Ground control was able to eject the reactor core into orbit before the rest of the satellite came crashing down and burnt up in earth's atmosphere. About four hundred and fifty miles above the earth's surface, the nuclear core was still circling the globe about every ninety-nine minutes but would eventually fall to earth—some time and some place.

18

Down in his eBay war room with a mug of Salada green tea, Brad couldn't get the New Orleans paper out of his mind. The president would be at Camp David in a couple of days. Camp David. *David.*

It reminded him of something in one of those coded auctions that he saw MealyMouth was involved in, one he hadn't fully analyzed yet. He called up the MealyMouth listings again and did a search for *David.*

Bingo! There it was. An auction for a soldering iron with two reels of tin and lead solder. The perfect thing for putting the final touches on some kind of lead container—making the thing absolutely, 100 percent sealed. If someone did acquire the radioactive hand of death or any other source much stronger than a tiny check source to make sure one's radiac meter was operating correctly in the presence of radiation, they would have to carry it in a lead-lined container or something similar to keep most of the radiation from escaping to the outside where it could be detected.

A check source was tiny, with very little radiation emitted and quite safe to living things, but when you turned on your radiac meter and brought a check source near, the radiac would start ticking like crazy. If you turned the radiac probe away and pointed to anywhere in the outside world, you would get the occasional tick from the normal background radiation, which was found everywhere in the universe—cosmic rays hitting the earth from outer space, uranium, radium, and countless other radioactive elements found naturally in the earth, radon gas, and so on. When you then pointed back to the tiny check source, it would again start ticking like crazy. That simple demonstration always impressed the heck out of kids in science class or even highly educated adults such as top politicians, allied military leaders, and other dignitaries visiting AFRRI and getting its famous tour and nuclear/radiological demonstrations.

Brad remembered the first time he taught his medical effects of nuclear weapons course at Kirtland Air Force Base in Albuquerque, New Mexico, at the Defense Nuclear Weapons School. As just one of countless demonstrations, he had a faculty member hide a hotter than usual test source. This was not the kind that could be bought by any middle school science teacher for kids to handle but a special military grade one for the real experts. Brad then monitored each group of students as they used a radiac to try and find the source in a small enclosed field used for rad training.

The students didn't know, but the instructor had hidden the source in a tiny lead box inside a rain barrel, placing it at about the height that a student would be holding his radiac scanning probe. The sides and bottom of this box were shielded with an inch of lead such that nothing emitted any stronger than normal background radiation. But the box lid was fully open, shooting a barrage of radioactive particles and rays straight up into the air, a veritable Disney-sized production of fireworks, except that none were visible to the naked eye.

That day Brad followed the first student group, its leader holding the probe out front as he walked, gradually scanning from left to right and back again. Nothing. Just the occasional *tick tick*. The moment the probe reached a point above the open box that contained the source, suddenly there burst forth a veritable explosion of atomic activity, and the radiac went crazy. It was like straining to hear a faint whisper and suddenly have booming thunder blast your eardrums to smithereens. The students nearly passed out and ran backward for cover. Brad was chagrinned to discover he also nearly jumped out of his shoes and walked backward as fast as he could.Ever since 9/11 potential targets of high value to terrorists—such as the entire Washington DC area, key transport hubs in cities such as New York, ports receiving tons of goods from overseas, etc.—were ringed with hidden radiation detectors. There were even specially trained law enforcement officers who drove in their squad cars installed with radiation detection equipment on all the highways and byways in an attempt to catch anyone trying to transport something radioactively dangerous without permission. All of the above would occasionally detect and apprehend some poor soul who had just left the radiation medicine department of a nearby hospital, where they had received into their bodies radioactive sources for various kinds of body scans or treatment of cancer. Such individuals normally had their hospital paperwork with them and could easily explain their condition and were promptly released, but it could still be a distressing experience.

Whoever MealyMouth was, he clearly appeared to know the score and realize that he couldn't get far with the radioactive hand of death unless it were tightly sealed in a lead or similar container that would prevent radiation significantly above background levels from being released. That would also keep the transporter from giving himself a fatal dose with such an intensely hot item.

So Brad studied closely the auction listing description for the lead soldering kit that MealyMouth wanted. It held the kind of rambling personal details that Brad was just beginning to suspect included coded plans. If he saw this kind of verbiage in an auction for a Hollywood movie on DVD or for a crate of picture frames, he would guess the dealer was just one of those long-winded, garrulous types who couldn't stop talking about himself. But if the item was the radioactive hand of death, this must mean something else. The item read:

> Folks, this auction is for a really neat soldering iron kit that includes two whole reels of lead solder. That's enough to seal up a lot of lead containers or reconnect some broken metal items around the house or patch your circuit board. I think you will really find this useful. I took my son David camping once, and we found it useful for just about everything. I think that was last February 3. Anyway, I took David camping, and we used it, but he did have one painful experience. You've got to be careful with

soldering irons—they get really hot on the tip, guys, so don't touch them! Be careful, or you can really get hurt! Okay?

Oh no!

Anyone coming at this item all by itself might read this simply as a chatty, roundabout way for the seller to warn of the risks in using his item. A naïve reader might not even notice the personal references and would just focus on the item details that interested him. But Brad was beginning to see a pattern in all the interrelated auctions that connected these guys. "David camping," which was said twice, had to mean "Camp David." February 3 this year was the day of the Camp David summit Brad noted in Dad's paper. Painful? Hot? Get hurt?

Was Brad crazy, or were these guys planning to kill the president at Camp David this coming weekend and disrupt the Middle East peace process, all with the radioactive hand of death being transported in a sealed lead container?

19

Brad went for a jog earlier than usual that afternoon. In fact, ever since his incident with the three goons in the white van atop Balmoral Ridge right at dusk, he had been sticking strictly to broad daylight and not gone much farther than about a mile in any one direction from home. He would go east for a bit then return and go the other direction for a mile and head back. Always in well-trafficked areas.

Sometimes he drove all the way to nearby Fort Detrick in Frederick just so he could run on the paved trails there within a secured area and enjoy being outdoors without feeling in danger.

When he got back to eBay after cooling down and cleaning up, he immediately checked on that auction, which he took to be for the radioactive hand of death. Earlier, using Dad's new account, he put a mere seventy-five dollar bid on the thing and was immediately outbid. Now he saw the bidding had gone way up to $323.71—yet the same cluster of buyers as before was involved. They were simply outbidding each other.

Hmm. I wonder if any of these other guys know each other or are in cahoots with each other. Let's just assume for a moment that at least two are. Likely all aren't, because anyone could see this and bid on it, just as Dad has done recently. How would the conspirators—brood members quite possibly, though it could be another group—respond to an interloper trying to take this item from them? Was one of the other current bidders an interloper that they were determined to outbid?

Brad did something crazy. He had never even considered something like this before. He was too loyal an eBayer to break the rules, but this was the time to do it. He entered a bid way higher than he or Dad could afford. If they won, Brad would be in a heap of trouble, because he wouldn't have the money to pay. But he had a strong feeling that one of the brood members, or possibly unrelated terrorist involved with this auction, would quickly outbid him, and he would be off the hook. That is, off the eBay hook for disobeying its rules...but quite possibly *on* the hook with the terrorists.

Brad entered a new bid for $5,002.97. No one could possibly bid that much on something described literally as simply an esselon chunk...unless, that is, he knew exactly what it was and absolutely had to have it to complete some plan.

Immediately the bid rose to over $5,010.

And MealyMouth was still in the lead.

Oh, yeah. This smells just like the brood. They already had it in for me for prior reasons, and now they would be eager to get rid of Cajun-Dad before he bankrupted them or even took their precious weapon away. If they could figure out who Cajun-Dad was, they would at least try to intimidate him...maybe eliminate him.

Brad had to warn Dad. He found him on Brad's own favorite chair watching a fishing show on TV, a small glass of bourbon in his hand.

"Dad, you remember a few days ago when you asked me how many guns were in the house?"

"Dat true. I axed when Ma said Crazy Joe and Billy Bupp, tey might be headed dis way."

"I've got a Smith and Wesson Model 19 Combat Magnum revolver. That's the one I used to catch the third terrorist last fall. And after we almost lost Mary Lou and the twins that day, I bought her a Remington .380 semi-auto pistol and taught her how to use it. It fits nice and sweet inside her purse."

"Dat magnum be a good pea-shooter, but de .380, that be just a little girl's gun. Dat be jes a cap pistol. Bullet bounce right off de gator and not even make 'im mad. Won' even feel it."

"Well, I'm not too worried about gators attacking her up here. It's people I'm concerned about, and their hides aren't nearly as tough. Besides, I taught her how to use it, too, and she's pretty good."

"You wasn't the first, son. I taught her to shoot when she was just two years old. By ta age o' three, she could shoot the left wing off a dragonfly from acrost the other side of the Ba-yoo wit her .22 and then shoot ta other wing when it tried to get away. When she was five I could point out a rain drop a hunnert yards up fallin' in a thunderstorm, and she could smash jes that one back inta steem with a .30 ought six before it hit ta groun'… without tetchin' any other raindrop! Dat girl, she could shoot the cockadoodledoo rite out de rooster's mouth without rufflin' his feathers. Wouldn't even be hurt! He'd stan' up dere on de fence post fluffin' aroun' tryin' ta crow and couldn't get it out! Why dat girl could, with both eyes shut, shoot a swamp sprite sittin' on the other side of a live oak, split the oak in half, and make a coffin outta it afore de sprite fell down daid rite inda middle of it."

"Dad, there's no such thing as swamp sprites."

"Not anymore! Not since she kilt 'em all! Why that girl can—"

"Dad, who are Crazy Joe and Billy Bupp, anyway?"

"Son, down on de ba-yoo dem gators are always looking for a meal. You catch yourself a fat and sassy catfish, and if you don' watch out, dem gators come snatch it away. You take you pirogue out and see dem gator eyes watchin' yoo. Alla time. Human flesh jes as tasty as fish. Dey likes Cajun flesh best of all cause they get so little of it. They see you pirogue, she slipping low in de water, dat gator gonna come sneakin' up on yoo, seein' if he can't get no snack! Maybe jes reach over the low edge and grab a bite outta yo arm. Worse yet, try to drag you outta de boat an' drown yoo and eat de whole t'ing when he ready."

"But who are those two fellows?"

"I'm gittin' ta dat! You gotta always give a good Cajun time ta talk, time ta gets it all out.

Down on de ba-yoo mos' everyone 'fraid of de gators. Even Cajun gotta be careful, keep de rifle or shotgun ready…jes in case. But down on de ba-yoo even de gators dey be afraid of Crazy Joe and Billy Bupp. Gators see dose two and clear out de whole area."

"Dad, you're lapsing into Cajun again, and Ma ain't—I mean *isn't*—even here."

"Not in body, son. But I can see her in my head. I can hear that siren song. Ain't no woman like a good Cajun woman."

"So who are those guys dat—*that*—scare even the alligators?"

"No one on the bayou ever see the likes of them before. They are something to stay away from. You see them coming, and you'd better get away fast. Your magnum won't mean anymore to them than if you was flinging a booger at 'em.

"Why dem boys is so strong three elephants couldn't stomp 'em down. You could stack de three right on top de Billy Bupp, an' he wouldna even buckle. Might sink inta de swamp a couple of feet but den he'd jes laugh, toss dem ellies aside, give a good sneeze, and pop up ten feet into de air!

"Why dem boys is so big dere ain't a building in all of St. Martin Parish big enough to hold 'em. Can't get through no doorway, not even on dey's hands 'n knees. Not even the big fire department doorway. Why dem boys is so fierce the whole British army still too scared ta come back into Cajun territory. Dem boys kicked 'em out in the Battle of N'awleens in 1816 'n they haven't dared come back since! Dem boys—"

"Dad, the Battle of New Orleans was in 1815."

"Not *this* 'un! In '15 twas just a warm-up. Just Andrew Jackson and a few regular Cajuns. Them fellows did a good enough job, but when the Brits came back de next year,

Crazy Joe and Billy Bupp finished it! Revenge for Acadia, ya know? And de redcoats ain't been back never since."

"Funny, but I don't remember anything in history about a Second Battle of New Orleans a year later."

"Course not! Had to leave Billy Bupp outa da history books so as not to scare de chillun's."

"And Crazy Joe, too?"

"Dat true. Why dem boys—"

Good grief. "Dad?"

"Yeah, son?"

"Nice talking to you, but I've got to get back to work now. Bye."

Seventy-Two Hours before the Wedding

Brad had no hard evidence to go on but had some strong suspicions that someone was plotting to attack the president at Camp David this coming weekend. Who could he warn? The Secret Service would be logical if he had solid proof, but without that, wouldn't they consider him a kook? It might take so much time to convince them that Brad was on the level that the thing would be over with one way or the other by then.

Brad knew only a small handful of people who currently worked in the White House and would probably listen to him and take the threat seriously. If he could convince them, they would certainly get a fair hearing with the Secret Service. Only a few weeks after 9/11 the chief of the White House medical staff had asked the president's science advisor for a recommendation of who could come to the White House to teach them about radiation risks and countermeasures. Dr. Barstow told them about AFRRI and Brad's work as the director of the medical effects of ionizing radiation course. Next thing Brad had an invitation to bring along his best two instructors and spend the day briefing them. At the end, the med staff chief had even talked about flying the AFRRI team back from the National Naval Medical Center helipad direct to the White House lawn in the event of a major radiological attack or incident to help contain the problem.

That man would take Brad seriously. He looked up the number in his files and called Commander Dan Jefferson. No answer, but he left a brief but succinct message on the phone machine.

Moments later, the phone rang, and Brad answered eagerly.

Not Jefferson.

"Major Stout? This is Deputy Lancer of the Frederick County Sheriff's office. We spoke a few days ago."

"Yes, I remember." *This can't be good.* Brad could feel his armpits getting moister.

"I rather thought you would. Major Stout, I'm afraid I have some very bad news for you. You have a sister named Victoria Stout, is that correct?"

"Yes, Officer." Brad's heart was thumping audibly now.

"And she's been on some kind of international Rhineland tour in France, Germany, and the Netherlands for the past couple of weeks?"

"Yes."

"Sir, I regret to inform you that INTERPOL has just called to say she has been kidnapped in Germany."

Brad swallowed hard and tried to keep breathing.

"Sir, are you still there?"

He cleared his throat. "Yes…I'm still here."

"I'm afraid there is more bad news for you on a different front. The third man in that white van that crashed over the Balmoral cliff has come out of his coma. The doctors say we can interview him tomorrow."

"What's that got to do with my sister? What's being done for her?"

"Sir, I know you must be worried, but INTERPOL and the German national police are on top of that. There isn't anyone better equipped to handle a case like this."

Brad had been to Germany many times in recent years; he believed that. "That's good."

"The point is, sir, we don't want you to even think about leaving town until we've had a chance to interview the crash victim. Do you understand what I'm saying?"

"Perfectly."

"Good, and believe me, we will keep you apprised of any developments in your sister's case as soon as we learn of them. You have our condolences, sir."

No sooner had Brad hung up the phone then it rang again.

Brad noted the caller ID. Still not Jefferson. *069. That's an overseas area code.*

A voice he didn't recognize, and it was muffled, as if the speaker had a cloth over the phone or something. "Stout?"

"This is he."

"We have your sister. You have the diary we want. Are you interested in talking about a trade, or shall we take her back to the Rhine for a one-way trip?"

Brad couldn't quite make out the accent. The man spoke in English and didn't have Germanic overtones. Maybe from somewhere in Eastern Europe.

"Sounds like a fair trade to me…so long as I get her back safe and sound."

"You are a reasonable man. She said you would be."

"How do I know you really have her? Put her on the phone."

"Not yet. Not today. I can give you her social security number, her birth date, her middle initial—"

"You could know all that just by stealing her purse."

"Oh, yeah, she said to tell you your cat is called TomTom the Third, and everyone called your father Pop. None of that is in her purse."

"So when and where do we trade?"

"You've got twenty-four hours to get to Landstuhl. We'll meet at the old Nanstein castle ruin on top of the hill. When you're ready, dial this number I'm going to give you."

Brad looked at his watch. "Your time zone is six hours ahead of mine. I make that to be 10:26 p.m. your time."

"Correct. See you then."

Brad hung up the phone. He was starting to tremble.

Mary Lou was drying dishes and came to the doorway with a plate and a dishrag. She took one look at Brad's face, and the dish slipped to the floor where it cracked into tiny pieces that sped across the linoleum. "Brad, what's the matter?"

He struggled for control. "Sweetie, remember when I told you Colonel Fukioki might pull something at the last minute before the wedding, just to give me a hard time?"

She nodded.

"Well I have to take the next flight from Dulles to Frankfurt."

"That's not fair! You're on two week's leave for the wedding and honeymoon. And it's just three days before the ceremony! Can you make it back in time?"

"I hope so. I'll do my best."

"Great galloping rattlesnake claws! First Ma got herself lost, Daddy's out of it half the time, and now you're leaving the country? Am I going to have to get married all by myself?"

"Sweetie, I am sorry. And I'll be back on time if it is humanly possible."

She started to cry and ran out of the room. He didn't have time to do anything, not even comfort her or pack. He had to move—*fast*. He had been on the Dulles/Frankfurt run many times to teach his course in Germany at the bases in Landstuhl, in Augsburg before it closed, at the NATO Headquarters Allied Force Command in Heidelberg, and elsewhere. He knew approximately the flight schedule without even looking it up. The last non-stop overnight flight of the day left around 10:00 p.m.

More importantly, he had lots of friends at all those bases, people who owed him favors, since he came whenever they needed him to provide the training crucial for their recertification. After booking his flight, he called the radiation control officer at Landstuhl Hospital. Following some foreshortened pleasantries, he came right to the point.

"Can you get me a blank toe tag from the hospital morgue? And a maximum dose of chloral hydrate? In two syringes? About two grams each should do it."

"Sure, Brad, that's a schedule six controlled substance back in the States but not in the UK and some other European countries. No problem. Just call me when you get in, and we'll see what else we can do. Chip's in town this week."

Ah, Chip! He will come in handy. He has everything. "That is great, Carl. Just super. I really appreciate your help. Could you ask Chip if he has night vision goggles handy? And see if he can get me a Mahkarov 9 mil, the old Stasi version."

"You got it, pal. Anything for a bud. You saved my ass last year when you got my whole team credentialed just in time to pass inspection. Saved my whole career just in the nick of time. By the way, Redman is still here, too. I know he'd be happy to help."

Redman. Fantastic. For the first time I think the odds are changing in my favor. "Oh, wow, is that good news. I figured he'd be back on greenie beanie duty by now."

"Nope, he's not scheduled to go back to a Special Forces group for another month."

"Good, good, good! Here's what I'd like to ask him to do for me—"

Moments later Brad was heading for his own front door at top speed. Just then Dad intercepted him.

"Brad, we've got a problem."

Brad started to snap but controlled it. "Yeah?"

"I just got an e-mail from a strange eBay character who calls himself MealyMouth. He warns me to back off the esselon chunk auction or else. What do you want me to do, keep bidding her up?"

"Dad, I'm leaving town for about thirty-six hours, so I think you'd better pull back from that auction like he says. And keep my magnum with you till I get back. It's in my nightstand. And please make sure Mary Lou keeps her .380 on her at all times. Tell her it looks like a replay of last fall coming up again."

"Son, I see that look in your eye again. It's killing time. Can I come with you?"

"Dad, I'd like nothing better, but Mary Lou needs you more right now. You're all she's got left."

Wedding Minus Sixty-Six Hours

Making a flight reservation just minutes before the flight was full meant Brad had to get the last, most crowded, most miserable seat in coach for the flight from Dulles to Frankfurt. In years past when he was lucky, he could use his frequent flyer miles to get a free upgrade to business class. He loved that luxury with the infinitely adjustable seats, the vibration feature, the greater free space, and the far superior food and wine selections.

But not this time. He ended up on the back row right next to the bulkhead, meaning his cheapie regular seat wouldn't recline back at all. He had a middle seat with large fellows on either side of him, and he could barely wedge his legs into the cramped space in front of him. He felt like he had been squeezed into a tissue box and knew he wouldn't get much rest this night.

Eight hours later they landed in Frankfurt. Brad made his way through the humongous airport to the exit and rented a car. He got onto the Autobahn A63 shortly thereafter and within seconds was flying at one hundred and sixty kilometers an hour—all quite legal on the

Autobahn, except in the areas near exits where slower speeds were posted.

He knew the way to Landstuhl without even consulting a map. He must have taken this route ten or twelve times in the past few years. *Why would this ex-Stasi group pick Landstuhl, anyway? Heidelberg made a better choice since that is right on the Rhine where they nabbed Victoria. If they wanted to get seventy or so miles away from the river, why did they pick a place that had an American army base? A place they've got to know I may have some connection? Or maybe they don't know as much about me as I think. Can it be they don't even know I'm in the army? They just think I'm a regular civilian with the diary?*

Certainly these thugs were ill-informed about the diary. Yes, Brad had acquired it a couple of months back at high cost at the end of a frantic auction. Later the brood member Cujo-man demanded it, paid for it, and Brad delivered it to him, but only as bait. That felon never had a chance to keep it, for the FBI had retained it as evidence when they captured him immediately upon delivery, and Brad hadn't even seen it since. His appeal to the court had been rejected.

If these ex-Stasi goons knew so little about that, maybe they knew very little about Brad, his strengths, connections, and fierce determination to take all of them out and save his sister or die in the attempt.

What would they do if they realized before he could defeat them all that he didn't even have the diary to trade in the first place?

And what on earth did they want with an old World War II diary written by an American spy masquerading as an SS officer in Munich in 1945? Brad had never had a chance to read the whole thing. He skimmed the first hundred pages or so, focused on the two sections about the Nazi effort to develop the atomic bomb, and never read the final portions at all. He couldn't imagine the Stasi being interested in the parts he had seen, not after all these decades. Was there something nearer the end that worried them? After all, Munich contained not only the SS headquarters, but also the HQ of the NSDAP, the National Socialists German Workers' Party.

Brad didn't know that non-military part of WWII history very well, but maybe the diary contained some secret that even today could cause trouble for surviving communists. Maybe names of people or a description of their deeds, things that could lead to prosecution or revenge even in the present. He knew, for example, that when the Berlin Wall went down in 1989 and the next year the two halves of Germany reunited, that the East German secret police were immediately out of a job. Worse yet for them, all their records, lists of undercover informants, and so on became exposed to the public. Plenty of the long-suffering German victims who had never been communists didn't wait for the law to exact revenge on the ex-Stasi and their informants. They took care of it themselves.

✕

Wedding Minus Fifty-Four Hours

It was great seeing Carl again, but Brad begged for a couple of hours sleep on the couch before implementing their plan. Carl doubtlessly understood, having himself often flown in from the States on an overnight flight…one's nighttime cut short by the time zone difference. Just when your body felt that it was *really* late, well past midnight in home time, you suddenly got off the plane, exhausted, to face a new dawn and a new *long* day in the new, very sunny time zone.

Besides, none of his three friends, Carl, Chip, and Redman, had yet had time to complete all their preparations and bring the pieces of the jigsaw back to Brad to assemble.

It was four hours later, and Brad woke up starving, just in time for a huge dinner with his friends. Plenty of wienerschnitzel, kartoffelsalat, schupfnudeln, und sauerkraut to go around as they worked out the details of their ground plan. Brad even allowed himself ein bier, Bitburger's Köstritzer Schwarzbier, his favorite.

Wedding Minus Fifty Hours

Redman was the code name for Staff Sergeant Brightfeather, the most renowned tracker in the US Army, famed for chasing Taliban high and low through the mountainous regions of Afghanistan and walking on pure rock where no one but an expert could exact a single trace. When he found one, Brightfeather would call it in, and a sniper team would close the gap, identify the turbaned target clinging to a boulder on the side of the cliff, and off him with a .50 cal in a tightly focused explosion of blood, rock fragments, and dust. Redman was one of the great-great grandsons of Ashishishe, General George Armstrong Custer's Crow tribe scout known to the Garryowen men as Curley and best known as the only army survivor of Custer's Last Stand at the suicidal Battle of Little Bighorn.

Redman was a green beret with the Tenth Special Forces Group operating out of Fort Carson, Colorado. He had been wounded on a secret mission in Afghanistan—a nearby buddy stepped on a mine, and fragments pierced Redman's thighs and torso also—and sent to the Landstuhl Regional Medical Center for treatment. He still had a couple of weeks of convalescent leave before returning to duty and physically wasn't in prime fighting shape at the moment. However, his tracking and scouting senses were undiminished, and he had been up on the castle mountainside since dark, his eagle eyes enhanced by night vision goggles, ascertaining the number and positions of the ex-Stasi kidnap team.

Still at Carl's house, Brad slipped his EXP Microphone M4 earphone and mouthpiece into position. He tapped rather than spoke to avoid giving the man away in case he were in a precarious moment at that instant and couldn't speak.

"Roger, Big Daddy."

That was the code name they all had jokingly given to Brad earlier at dinner when they learned he was about to become a husband and father.

"Redman, what's your count?"

"Their lead man arrived on foot hours ago. He's guarding the front gate to the castle. Once all the tourists left, he slipped the caretaker some cash to leave the gate unlocked. About thirty minutes ago a small, dark sedan—a late model Opel Vectra—arrived and is still in the parking lot. There were three men. The driver stayed with the car. It is pointed out for a possibly quick getaway. That means the driver can't see much of the action while sitting in his seat.

"The other two men exited the vehicle and took their positions. The first one is standing on the highest turret of the guard tower, near the gift shop and cafe, where he has a view of the sheer drop of the main castle wall and the main approach from the valley. The other is standing near the gate watching the path up from the parking lot."

"Anyone with NVG?"

"Only the one on the turret, as far as I have seen. Could be more sets in the car, but no one else is carrying them. The moon is nearly full, and you can see pretty well in any of the open spaces unaided. It's just in the shadows where it seems really dark."

"Good, good. Thanks. How are you holding up in the cold out there?"

"Freezing my rocks off. I've lost too much muscle since spending six weeks in the hospital. I haven't lifted more than three hundred pounds since before I got creamed."

"Sorry, buddy. When this is over, I'll buy you the biggest hot chocolate you've ever seen."

Redman laughed in a low, whispery voice.

"Any sign of Queenie?"

That was Victoria's code name.

"Negative. She couldn't possibly be in that small sedan, not with the three burly thugs who were in that. However, she could be in the control van at the base of the mountain. Roonie's been watching that since it arrived."

That was Chip's code name.

"I'll check in with him in a minute. Anything else I need to know from you first? What are they wearing? Any camo paint on their faces?"

"Negative on the camo. Standard civvies for a cold night like this. Thick, dark coats, gloves, and wool pullover caps. Nothing looks military."

"Owe you big time, buddy. Thanks."

Brad tapped the speaker twice.

"Roger, Big Daddy," came Roonie's voice.

"You've got eyes on the van, I hear. What do they see?"

"It arrived about an hour before the sedan up on the mountain. Parked on Schlossstrasse. A Mercedes Benz, closed-box style minivan. Big three-seater. I think it's a Sprinter 213. All I can see clearly is a driver and a second guy riding shotgun. They parked on the edge of the town about half a block from the turnoff to come up the mountain, angled where they can see anyone getting on or off that road."

"Do you think there are any other vehicles or guys on foot involved?"

"Anything is possible, but neither Redman nor I have spotted anybody else. And their opsec is pretty low key. They aren't running this like a high intel operation; more like a sloppy bunch of criminals who think muscles and guns will win the day. I don't think they have any idea what they are up against."

"Any sign of Queenie?"

"Can't be sure. When I switched to infrared I got readings on a third person in the back of the van, but I don't know if it's her or one of the thugs. Is Queenie a large person?"

"Taller than average but quite thin."

"Let me try again from a different angle. Gimme me a minute to change position."

"Roger that."

Moments later. "Big Daddy?"

"Here."

"Inconclusive. Infrared signature is a little smaller than the thugs in front. But I can't tell if number three is sitting up or lying on the seat curled up. I think the latter."

"That would be consistent with a prisoner tied up and lying on the back seat." Brad's blood boiled at the thought of his sister being manhandled by these gunsels tying her up and tossing her into the back seat. He wanted to rip their livers out and stuff them down their throats. *Scratch that! Got to keep a clear head and keep emotion out of it till this is over. You're in the army, Stout. Act like it. Eyes solely on the mission!*

"Don't exclude the possibility of the group leader in the back taking it easy while his minions do all the work."

"Point taken. Let's not accept any theories or assumptions until we can verify them. Owe you big time, Roonie. Out here."

"Out."

Still in the house, Brad turned to Carl, code name Vinnie. "Time to move out. Let's do this thing, buddy."

In Brad's rental car, Vinnie drove the two of them off base and slowly through the German town of Landstuhl in the valley between the hill for the base and that for the castle ruins. Both men kept sharp eyes out for any other vehicles or pedestrians who seemed out of the ordinary or a possible threat.

Nothing stood out. Mostly a few women who appeared to be wrapping up their shopping, plenty of people entering or leaving the many restaurants ringing the town square, a handful of people heading for the lone cinema on this side of town.

Brad ducked under the window of his seat as Vinnie drove him past the large gangster van and entered Burgweg, the steep and winding road leading up the castle hill.

Vinnie kept a sharp eye out here as well, in case others were hidden in the woods that lay thick at the base but thinned out as the hill rose. He slowed to a crawl just as the road became a dark, shadowy patch on the back side of the castle.

"Now, Big Daddy."

"Give me five minutes to get in."

Brad opened his door with one hand, held his pack in the other, and rolled out of the slowly moving vehicle onto the road, landing with an unpleasant bump but continuing to roll to the side of the road, dispersing the force of impact. He looked up the hillside some hundred feet to the base of the castle. With the bright moon on the far side, the ancient stones of the walls and parapets reminded him of too many Dracula movies he watched during his youth. He could almost imagine old Vlad creeping like an enormous cockroach straight down the stone wall to meet him face to face as he came up.

He shuddered. Soon he was panting but trying to keep the sound low as he clambered through the brush to the base of the wall. A hundred yards to his left, he could see Vinnie in Brad's own rental sedan, headlights still on, paused before the final turn to the parking lot.

23

Wedding Minus Forty-Nine Hours

Brad took his pack off, extracted the grappling hook and rope, and quietly as possible threw it over a section of thirty-foot high wall of the twelfth century castle. He easily got a good grip with the hook, for this castle was in ruins with rough, broken stone along the ramparts rather than smooth masonry. He donned his pack, checked the tension in the rope, then started clambering up…trying to stay silent as possible. He knew from Redman's report that a lookout stood at the highest point on the far wall.

It was tough going, and within seconds Brad was panting, trying to suppress the sound. He hadn't done anything like this in a few years, not since he took the Army Medical Department Officers Advanced Course at Fort Sam Houston in San Antonio, particularly when they went out on field exercises at nearby Camp Bullis.

Further, his hands still hurt from the encounter on Balmoral Ridge with the goons whom he took to be part of this same group here in Landstuhl. Over the preceding days, his hands had largely healed, and most of the bandages were gone, but he still had streaks of scabs at the sites of the worst scrapes, and his hands felt tender all over from the force exerted against that sapling and the rocks at the cliff edge. Wearing Metolius rock climbing gloves tonight helped.

Finally he reached the top. Bent over, he crept into the shadows of a battlement where he couldn't be seen easily, got the night vision goggles out of his pack, and put them on. He always enjoyed using these, especially on the many night helicopter flights at Fort Rucker a few years ago. There was a cool dream-like quality seeing everything in a kind of green glow.

Yep, he easily spotted the lookout on the far wall about thirty to forty yards away. The guy was scouring that side of the cliff, that wall guarding the main route of access in the old days when the place was built. Like Roonie said, their opsec was fairly low key. Brad now looked carefully through the interior courtyard of the castle, just to make sure no one else had slipped into here to enjoy the party without being detected by his friends outside.

No one. Nothing but a couple of cats doing their rounds, looking for rodents. Probably belonged to the caretaker. Gingerly he made his way down the piles of rocks that lay strewn about. Centuries ago entire walls and sections of the bailey and countless merlons had collapsed into piles of rubble, and the place had never been fully restored, except for the paths tourists were supposed to stick to when touring the place.

He had been here several times before in recent years and figured the best place to set up his HQ would be the remains of the underground armory and storage tunnels. The roof of the armory, which doubled as the part of the floor in the castle courtyard, had long since collapsed into rubble. It was largely a hole in the ground now. Brad had in mind capturing one of these thugs alive—any of them would do—and using the drugs in his pack to make him talk.

He carefully crept down the mounds of fallen stone and found a shadowy corner at the bottom of the armory, put down his pack and NVG set, and started to signal his friends he was in position.

"Welcome, Mr. Stout. I've been expecting you. You're right on time."

He whirled to see the barrel of a pistol, not five feet away, pointed right at his face!

24

Wedding Minus Forty-Eight Hours

He was a big man with a cruel sneer on his face, an expression silently screaming "Aha! Now I've got you, you miserable little SOB!" It looked like a Mahkarov 9 mil pistol in his hand, just like the one holstered on Brad's web belt.

"I presume you've got the diary in that pack?"

"Of course," Brad lied. *This guy doesn't have a clue yet that Carl, pretending to be me and carrying a fake diary, should be walking slowly toward the castle front gate at this very moment.*

"Let's see it...and don't try anything. I've killed seven men with this pistol...most from greater distances than this, and sometimes when they were running."

Brad looked at the pistol, and the man retracted his arm back toward his waist. The mark of a professional. An amateur would keep the gun at arm's length, making a psychological barrier between the intruder and himself but also making him far more susceptible to being disarmed by a couple of quick kicks or chops by the target.

"Where's my sister?"

"She's fine."

"She'd better be. I said *where* is she?"

"Not far away."

"I want to see her before I give you the diary."

The man gave a sudden guttural laugh, almost a kind of grunt. "You are now in no position to bargain."

"You promised me on the phone you'd let me hear from my sister when I got here."

"You're right. I did. And I always keep my promises… even to miserable scum like you who killed two of my friends last week."

"I never laid a hand on any of them. Check the police reports. They had a vehicle accident."

"Yeah, right. Just by coincidence while they were after you. I'm not stupid, Mr. Stout."

'Mr. Stout,' he said. Not Major or Dr. but Mr. These guys can't be with the brood, at least not the Frederick branch. That brood knew everything about me.

"I may be many things but not stupid. I haven't survived this many years since the Wall fell by being a fool."

The Berlin Wall! This guy must be ex-Stasi like I first thought…if not some other kind of commie agent. "I'm not cooperating further until I hear from Victoria."

The man reached carefully into a pocket with his left hand and pulled out a small cassette player. He tossed it to Brad.

Brad caught it and pushed the play button. It was his sister's voice, a little shaky but not panicked. "Sorry, Brad. What a way to finish a great trip. Wish Pop could be here instead of you. Pop always knew what to do."

Pop. His answer to everything was fists and rage. Violence from beginning to end. Vicky's telling me to take these guys apart and not worry about the risk to her. Her trip is fin-ished. Maybe she realized she would be a goner no matter what. Maybe she was already gone. But she wanted me to take out her attackers regardless of any other consideration.

Brad felt his warrior spirit rising, taking over. Till now he had kept this as a military mission. Now it was per-sonal. No more than one person was going to leave this open hole of a castle armory alive. No more than one.

"Okay, so you had her. But this tape is at least a day old, I'll wager. I want proof she's alive now."

"Forget it schweinhund! Now get me that diary."

Brad noticed one of the caretaker's cats darting about in the corner behind the man, probably chasing a mouse.

Brad wasn't known for his acting ability, but he tried to force his eyes wide open and look terrified. "I always heard this place was haunted but didn't want to believe it. Gott in Himmel! There's a Rougarou rising up from the shadows behind you!" Brad backed up to the wall behind him as if terrified and grasped two loose rocks in the wall, one in each hand.

The man looked grim and determined and kept his gun on Brad but couldn't help himself from falling back a step. "Don't try to pull a corny stunt like that on me!"

"There! Behind you! He's opening his jaws! I can't watch!"

"I said shut up!"

"Can't you hear him? He's right on top of you! See?" Brad pretended to point in horror but launched the smaller rock at the poor cat a dozen feet away.

The cat yelped in one of those hair-raising cries that sounds like a small kid trapped in a well. He jumped into the air then scratched at the rocks when he landed, just like a monster scratching on dry bone.

The gunsel couldn't help himself from twisting around to see and falling into a crouch.

In two great bounds forward, Brad stood over him and clobbered him on his left temple with the larger rock, hard as he could.

The man crumpled.

Brad ripped the pistol out of the man's hands, hearing the crunch of a broken finger as he did. For good measure he whalloped him with the pistol on the right temple.

He tapped his radio once for Redman and thrice for Vinnie. "I've got the ring leader in the armory. Take out all four guys at the castle. All of them! Easy or hard, it's up to them."

He tapped twice for Roonie. "We're cleaning out the castle. Don't make a move on the van unless they try to leave or appear to be about to harm whoever's in the back."

A barely audible *pfft!* not far away sounded out as his friends went about their work as silently as possible.

$$\times$$

Brad took his grappling rope and tied up the ringleader as tight as he could.

"Big Daddy," her heard in his earphone. *Redman.*
"Yes?"

"Tower man down. Way down. Took a head shot and fell off then tumbled a hundred yards or more down the hill."

"How about the two at the gate?"

"They're looking around as if unsure what happened. Tower guy didn't cry out, and my silencer is pretty good."

Vinnie tapped in. "Big Daddy, the sedan driver surrendered. We have a prisoner."

"Good. Redman, can you handle the other two by yourself?"

"With both hands tied behind my back."

Brad kept his eye on his prisoner and waited anxiously for the next report.

Two agonizing minutes later, it came.

"Redman here. One more prisoner. I crept up behind the first guy and knocked him out before he realized I was there. But the second guy saw it, and I had to ice him when he reached for his gun. Used my SOG Tigershark knife."

Brad couldn't help wincing at the thought of that fourteen-inch combat-sharp blade cutting in. *I'll bet those guys are starting to understand how Custer felt. This is their last stand.*

"Please give your prisoner to Vinnie at the sedan. Then join me here in the armory."

"Roger."

Brad's prisoner was moaning and starting to come awake. Brad went to his pack and pulled out a battery-powered lantern, which he turned on to illuminate the fairly small space of the armory. It cast eerie shadows behind the various piles of rubble. He looked over to make sure the cat was all right, but he was long gone. *Probably more scared than hurt. Least I hope so.* TomTom wouldn't like it if he knew Brad had hurt a fellow cat.

Then Brad pulled out the two syringes of chloral hydrate and returned to the prisoner.

Redman silently joined Brad as the gunsel regained consciousness.

At first the thug looked terrified but then struggled to control his emotional expression.

Brad spoke first. "*Now* am I in a position to negotiate?"

No response.

"Where is my sister?"

Nothing.

"You're ex-Stasi, right?"

No response, but Brad took his furtive glance away from him as confirmation.

"I told you the truth when I said I never laid a hand on your friends who chased me back in America. They crashed because of their own stupidity as they tried to ram into me."

Still nothing.

"I know how you Stasi used to interrogate prisoners. I know you've got the blood and pain of scores, maybe hundreds on your conscience. But we Americans aren't like that. I'm not going to torture you."

The man looked relieved.

"I'm just going to inject you with the deadliest poison known to man," he lied.

Chlorate hydrate was often used as a recreational drug for getting high, but Brad didn't tell him that was in the syringe. It was a *maximum* safe dose, though, and would give him dizzy, sick-drunk feelings in a few moments and a heckuva hangover the next day...if he lived that long.

Brad bent over and stuck it in the neck, careful to miss the carotid artery, and shot the full dose in. "This other one"—he held up the second syringe—"is the antidote."

The man's eyes flew wide.

"You talk inside of the next one hundred and twenty seconds, I'll give you the antidote in time. Wait longer than that, and you won't be able to talk. It'll be too late. Now where's my sister?"

The man shook his head again, but this time with a tight, twisted turn of the neck where the veins now bulged.

"One hundred seconds left. First you'll feel a little light-headed. Then your heart will begin to pound. Then a little queasiness in your stomach. Eighty-five seconds."

As Brad mentioned each organ and symptom, the man tried to look toward that part, and the increasing panic in his eyes confirmed he experienced what Brad warned.

"Seventy seconds. Soon you'll experience some serious nausea."

The man gagged in confirmation.

"Dizziness next. Fifty-two seconds left. The dizziness will get a lot worse—your head will be spinning soon. Almost out of time. Forty seconds. *Where's my sister?*" he barked in his loudest, most ominous tone and moved in abruptly as if to strike.

Still nothing.

"Thirty seconds. Soon you will feel drowsy. It will get worse. You'll be too weak and sleepy even to lift a finger. End game coming. Twenty-two seconds."

Brad was starting to worry the man would call his bluff. The last thing on earth he wanted to do was any deliberate rough stuff. He just wanted his sister back, and this was the most merciful way he could think of to get the info he needed.

"Fifteen seconds—last chance! The drowsiness will lead to paralysis, and you'll die. But not right away. You'll linger for weeks still alive. Maybe we'll just hide you down here for those weeks. Got your toe tag ready right here." He brandished it.

"Nine, eight, seven, six, five—"

The man snapped something, gritted his teeth, jerked all his limbs, and went rigid, his face turning blue.

Redman bounded forward and sniffed the air. "Like toasted almonds."

"Cyanide capsule," concluded Brad. "Do *ex*-agents do things like that a dozen years after disbanding?"

Wedding Minus Forty-Seven Hours

Brad tapped into Vinnie's line. "Ringleader down. Please hold your two prisoners there while Redman and I join Roonie and find out if Queenie is in that van at the bottom of the hill. If she's not, we'll be needing to have a long talk with your prisoners."

"Roger."

Brad tapped into Roonie. "Any van activity?"

"Negative."

"Don't make a move unless you need to. Redman and I are on the way."

Brad and his special forces friend clambered out of the rock-strewn armory, ran across the ruined courtyard, out the gate, and down to the parking lot, where they noted Vinnie with the Stasi sedan, both prisoners now handcuffed to the steering wheel, the second still unconscious, it appeared.

"Keys in the ignition!" Vinnie stated as Brad and Redman darted over to the airport rental.

Brad drove, lights off, to avoid signaling the thugs in the van. Inside two minutes they were nearing the base of the hill, and Brad figured the parked van was about a hundred yards away. He pulled his car to the side of the road and turned it off.

Brad pulled out his Mahkarov. At a time like this he would rather have his old Army .45 Colt or the .357 magnum he kept at home. He only wanted the Stasi weapon to begin with as part of his original plan to masquerade as a Stasi agent himself, coming up from behind the men in the castle as if one of them at the precise moment that Vinnie would amble up, pretending to be Brad. But the ringleader's surprise move had squelched that plan.

Redman pulled his Tigershark knife out of the sheath, the silvery metal shining in the bright moonlight except for shadowy patches, which Brad, in one quick glance, assumed were bloodstains.

As they ran, Brad tapped into Roonie, "We're here. Hold your position then cover us as we move in. Redman will get the driver, I'll get the shotgunner, and then we'll find out who is in the back of that van."

"Roger. There's still no motion in the van. I think they're about to fall asleep."

Bent over, running silently, the two men split, running up from the back of the van toward the front.

Redman got there one pace ahead of Brad. He abruptly jerked open the driver door, reached in with a mighty left paw, and grabbed the scalp, pulling the man's head into the gleaming blade, which sliced deep and quick, left to right.

Brad opened the shotgun door just in time to see spurts of blood from the two torn carotid arteries of the driver startle and wake up the half-asleep guard.

Brad pressed the barrel mouth against the man's temple and barked, "Hände hoch!"

The confused man raised his hands as instructed by Brad in German.

Roonie arrived an instant later, grabbed the man's arms, and jerked him rudely from the vehicle, casting him upon the pavement face down and cuffed him, hands behind his back.

No resistance.

Brad tore open the side door.

26

It was Victoria! Bound and gagged, but was she alive?

Brad put two fingers against the side of her neck. Good, strong pulse. He noted her breathing was low and soft but regular. Drugged?

He tore off her binds and gag and stretched her out from her curled up position along the back seat. "Victoria, can you hear me? Wake up!"

No response.

He felt the pulse at her wrist. Strong and steady.

He pulled a penlight out of his webgear, turned it on, then gently with the other hand pulled open her left eyelid and shone the light in. Immediately the wide-open pupil began to shrink.

Good pupillary response. She's been sedated but not poisoned. I think she'll be okay.

Brad tapped into Vinnie's line. "Victim recovered alive. Drugged but alive. Are your prisoners still secure?"

"Roger."

"Vinnie, keep listening while I talk to Redman and Roonie here in person." Brad looked at his watch. "Dear friends, I owe you my life and my sister's life. I swear I will make it up to you another day. But can you live with this? I was never here. I've been in America all this time. Somehow just you three caught onto a presumed Red Army Faction splinter group plot and rescued the kidnapped family member of a US military serviceman. You killed two terrorists on the hill and one in the van. The ringleader committed suicide in the castle when his plan fell apart. You're going to call INTERPOL and the Bundespolizei and turn in three captured terrorists."

"Jawohl. Ich verstehe," said Redman.

Roonie nodded.

"What about your sister?" asked Vinnie over the radio.

"You guys did it. I was never here. Just take her up to the Army MEDCEN, and please see if you can get a toxicology analysis. I'd like to know what they dosed her with to see if there could be lingering results."

Redman and Roonie looked at each other and shrugged.

Brad said, his eyes glistening a bit in the moonlight, "Guys, I feel like we are now the four musketeers. For life! I really do. Or maybe Parzival and his three noble knights. But right now I've got to rush back to the States to try to save the president."

Brad left the remainder of the equipment they had brought with them on the pavement beside the van. "Auf wiedersehen, meine freunde. All for one, and one for all!"

He dashed back to his vehicle and sped off into the dark night for Frankfurt.

Wedding Minus Forty-Five Hours

At Frankfurt Airport, Brad discovered he was in luck. For the return trip on the first flight of the day he got a free upgrade to business class. No more super-cramped seat. Maybe he could get some sleep. Best of all, in the hour he had left before flight time, he could check e-mail in their business center and try again to get in touch with Commander Jefferson at the White House. They would likely be leaving soon for Camp David, including the good doctor, since the president never travelled anywhere without the head of the medical team.

In Lufthansa Business Lounge at the airport, Brad felt grateful for the cold bottle of good Warsteiner Pilsner that the hostess offered him. This late the place wasn't crowded, and he found a comfortable desk with a computer right away.

Scores of office emails. Mostly routine stuff. From his e-files he looked up the e-mail address of Commander Jefferson and sent an e-mail.

> Been trying to reach you by phone. I have reason to suspect an attempted terrorist attack at Camp David this weekend. You remember the

subject I taught you about fourteen months ago? This could be one of *those* kinds of attack. Please alert the secret service.

Next Brad checked out eBay. No surprise to find that MealyMouth had won the auction for the radioactive hand of death. As warned to do by MealyMouth, and encouraged to acquiesce to by Brad, Dad pulled back and didn't bid any higher. Neither did anyone else. The high bidder got it for a bit over five thousand dollars, likely had already paid by now and received the merchandise, since the seller was from western Maryland.

Brad e-mailed Dad to let the older man know who won that auction, in case he wasn't tracking it on his own. He also told Dad he'd be home soon and to please get ready the plans they had earlier set in motion.

He e-mailed Mary Lou to tell her how much he loved her and how he was at the airport and should be home again in about twelve hours.

Then, feeling the most relaxed in days, Brad sauntered down to the nearest duty free shop to buy Mary Lou an expensive bottle of perfume. Maybe that would help her forgive him for running out on her without much explanation three days before the wedding. Especially while she was still crying.

Perfume, perfume everywhere. So many choices. Nice to be able to take my time in making a decision, one that doesn't have life or death consequences.

He couldn't find anything by test scent that suggested Louisiana or the bayous. But as soon as he saw the name of this one, he couldn't resist: J'adore L'Absolu perfume by Christian Dior. The perfect message to send her in French. "I adore you absolutely."

Oh, yeah.

Wedding Minus Thirty-Four Hours

As Brad exited the plane at Dulles Airport, he passed the huge TV mounted over a row of seats at his gate. "This just in," said the newsman on CNN, "a spokesman from the INTERPOL National Central Bureau in Wiesbaden announced that the German Bundespolizei have disrupted the terrorist plot of a resurrected splinter group of the Red Army Faction, long thought to have been dissolved in 1998. With the assistance of some US Army soldiers from nearby Landstuhl Army base, a kidnap victim was freed, and the entire gang was captured or killed. The victim, an as yet unnamed American citizen, was kidnapped during a stopover in Heidelberg for the Rhine River cruise she was on. She has been admitted to the Landstuhl Medical Center and is expected to make a full recovery. The three soldiers have each been given a ten thousand euro reward by the cruise line."

Brad grinned. All in a day's work. And a nice reward to boot. Now he didn't feel so bad about not hanging around a few days, showing them all a good time.

28

Wedding Minus Thirty-One Hours

Brad drove up his driveway and immediately noted an odd brown patch in the thin snow covering his front yard. He parked and walked over to have a look. It lay only about ten yards from the front of the house.

The snow was only a couple of inches deep, and the top layer had melted some during the previous day then frozen overnight to leave a thin coat of ice. But here was a circular patch with no snow or ice, about a yard in diameter. Even the underlying brown grass was gone, and all that was left was dirt. Just dirt. At the center of the patch was a small crater, maybe three to four inches deep.

I'll have to ask Dad about this. Did he do it? Some kind of Cajun ritual before a wedding or something? Looked kind of like the remains of a small bonfire except there was no ash about.

Brad no sooner opened his front door upon return before the phone rang. He darted to it. "Hello?"

Strange pause on the other end. "Uh, Major Stout?"

"Yes."

"This is Deputy Lancer of the Frederick County Sheriff's Department. I didn't really expect you to be there."

"You called me, Deputy. What can I do for you?"

"Well, sir. I'm really glad you're there, because I've got some good news for you."

"I could sure use it."

"INTERPOL called again, and your sister has been rescued—unharmed!"

"Oh, deputy, that is wonderful news. I was so worried after you called before. Where is she?"

"She's in Landstuhl, Germany, at the army medical center. It's in all the news."

"Oh, well I haven't turned on the house TV today yet. The hospital, you say? Is she okay?"

"Yes, sir. Just drugged by the kidnapers, and she's staying a day or two for observation. But let me hasten to add that the kidnappers did not abuse or molest her in anyway."

"Wow, thank God for that! That is a big relief."

"So…you know…three army guys got rewards from the cruise line for effecting the rescue. Earlier reports mentioned a fourth man but somehow he…vanished. But I don't suppose you know anything?"

"That does sound mysterious, Deputy. But the main thing is that my sister is free and unharmed, isn't it?"

"Uh…well…yes, of course. I have some more good news for you, sir."

"Yes?"

"Getting back to that van crash on Balmoral Ridge a week ago. The only survivor came out of his coma, and we interviewed him in depth just this morning."

Brad held his breath and watched as Mary Lou came down the stairs, caught sight of him, and came over, beaming from ear to ear to hug him tight.

"You're back!" she whispered, burying her face in his chest. "Just in time! Just like you promised!"

"Well, you see, sir," continued Lancer on the phone, "he confirmed just what you told us earlier. Just a pure accident. He claimed he never saw you nor anyone else up on that ridge."

"That is good news. You know, generally you can take a military officer's word at face value. Most of us say exactly what we mean and mean what we say."

"Yes, sir, exactly. I do understand. In fact, when I briefed the sheriff about all this, he told me in no uncertain terms not to bother you any more. He said you are the one who stopped that dirty bomb plot last fall and killed or captured a bunch of terrorists. Pretty much all by yourself. I'm sorry, sir, I really am. I'm new to these parts and didn't realize you were the same man. My sheriff, he says you are a real hero. The genuine article."

"Thank you, Deputy. I appreciate your openness and honesty. I do."

"So anyway, sir. You can forget about what I said earlier. You are now free to leave town or do anything else you want."

"Well that's a relief. I do hate being tied to one spot when I need to travel in my job so much."

"Yes, sir. I think I understand. Anyway, we consider this case closed, at least as far as you are concerned. The third man in the van—all of them, really—led to some pretty interesting rap sheets when we ran their prints. I don't think anyone good and decent will miss any of those guys. Two dead, and the live one will likely spend the rest of his life behind bars."

"That is good to know. I'd hate to see innocent people die in a horrible wreck like that."

"So, sir, once again my apologies. And best of luck with whatever you may get involved with next. And if you ever need my help with…things of that nature…it would be an honor to work with you on something like that. It really would."

"Deputy Lancer, you have my lasting gratitude. I can see you are a man able to distinguish what's right from mere rules. Good-bye."

Brad dropped the phone, and it only half landed on the receiver. He swept Mary Lou up in his arms, her feet right off the floor, and kissed her gently beside her left eye, followed by a series of soft kisses down that cheek, across the chin, up the right cheek, and a final one beside her right eye. Her lashes tickled his lips.

She whispered, "You know I like butterfly kisses as much as the next girl, but I think you can do better than that."

He lifted her up another couple of inches till they were exactly face to face, eye to eye, mouth to mouth. Then he gave her a series of kisses, exploring her lips, her mouth, deeper and stronger and longer each time. Within seconds he felt like he would explode, and by her panting and huge, wide open pupils, he guessed she would, too.

"Is Dad in the house?"

"No, he went for a long walk. Left just before you got home."

"Good." Brad picked her up, noting she was heavier than last time, and headed for the bedroom. "He better not come back too soon."

He lay her softly on the bed then returned to the door and locked it. He looked back at her. Luscious, absolutely luscious. He hadn't even given her the perfume yet, but its name fit perfectly. "J'adore, Mary Lou. Absolument!"

"Moi aussi." She purred, lying back on the bed and opening her arms.

Even though it was freezing outside, the sheets were damp with sweat. Brad felt on top of the world. He and the other musketeers had saved his sister, he was no longer in trouble with the county mounties, and he had just spent the most wonderful hour imaginable with the loveliest girl in the world.

He turned to her. They were now like one. It seemed even their scent was now the same. Not two separate individuals joining occasionally simply for a frolic. Rather, one united whole. Two halves of one.

"What is it about pregnancy that makes you so completely insatiable?"

She smiled and tucked her head under his chin, tickling it with her rich, brown hair. "Oh, I'm satiated. Believe me, I am satiated."

He stroked the back of her head.

"Now tomorrow," she continued. "That's different. That will be our first night together officially as man and wife. And you ain't seen nothing yet. I've been holding back till then. You just wait till I get hold of you tomorrow night!"

"Holding back? You just sent me to the moon. What's tomorrow? Mars?"

"Further than that. Better than that. You'll see."

Brad could hear someone opening the front door and stomping in. Seemed to be deliberately making as much noise as possible.

"Hullo! Anybody home? I saw Brad's car, so I figured I'd better keep walking for another hour. But listen, guys, it is cold out there! This here is a Cajun body used to the steamy swamps. I can only take so much cold. I think I lost my rocks out there after the third mile."

The two of them scrambled to jump out of bed, throw on their clothes, and push their hair back into place. No time to comb or brush it.

"It's okay, Dad!" yelled Brad through the locked door. "We'll be out in a minute. Pour yourself a drink and warm up next to the heating vent."

"Now dat a good plan! Pee-aire, he lak dat!"

Struggling to get both legs down his pants, Brad turned to Mary Lou. "Sweetie, while I was gone, did I get a call from a Commander Jefferson at the White House?"

"You sure did." She was trying to get her bra back on, and for a moment Brad had a different idea about how to spend the next quarter hour. "I left the phone message on the machine for you."

Duty calls. He went to the phone and listened.

"Brad? This is Dan Jefferson…calling you back. I appreciate your message. I did inform the secret service immediately, but they said not to worry. This is a very important meeting, and they said security will be the tightest it has ever been in history. They said nothing can go wrong, so please don't worry. If you get any specific information about a possible threat, just leave a message with my service, and they'll get it to me. But I will shortly be closing down this line and not be reachable directly after we leave. Thanks, Brad."

Nothing can go wrong?

It reminded Brad of the old joke about people onboard a new plane. As it took off, this message came across the loudspeaker: "Ladies and gentlemen, welcome to the first ever totally automated, unpiloted flight. Don't be concerned, nothing possible can go wrong…can go wrong… can go wrong…"

Wedding Minus Twenty-Eight Hours

Brad and Mary Lou were sitting at the kitchen table, enjoying tea and coffee and each other's company, talking about the final details of the wedding, when Brad felt the time was right to ask a question that had been on his mind for some time.

"Sweetie, your dad said something about Ma having a charm necklace made out of animal parts. Is that for real?"

"Sure is. It has some part of every type of animal that she has ever personally killed. It's got that gator penis and chicken foot, like you've already heard. Then an armadillo tail, squirrel skull, dove wishbone, rabbit foot, chunk of deer antler, end segment of a possum tail, a bit of raccoon scalp, a fox claw, a rattlesnake rattle, something from a wolverine. An owl beak—"

"She killed an owl? I thought you Cajuns revered owls."

"Oh, not on purpose. She was driving fast one night, and her headlights must have blinded it. It flew right into the front of her pickup truck."

"Oh, that's better, then. What else?"

"A coyote foot, cottonmouth fangs, a woodcock feather, dried pelican lip, a scale from a giant alligator gar, falcon claw, sturgeon fin, small turtle shell, mouse tail, rat whiskers, bat wing, crawfish main claw, piece of an oyster shell, dried salamander leg, weasel claw, catfish whisker, porcupine quill, woodpecker beak, dried bullfrog croaker... I forget the rest, but it's something like eighty to one hundred pieces all told. If you ask her some time, she can tell you—or show you—the rest."

"Good grief! She must look a sight when wearing that thing!"

She giggled. "Well, everything's been properly sun-dried or tanned and doesn't smell...much. And she doesn't usually wear it. Just on special occasions like church picnics where she wants to look her best. The rest of the time it hangs out in the shed."

"Special occasions? You don't mean like—"

"Oh, no! Not for the wedding. I told her no way she could bring it up here."

"Well, that's a relief. Is she really as superstitious as she comes across? I mean, I haven't even met her yet and just talked with her on the phone for about half a minute, but I've got this image of her as almost a mythological figure, kind of like a sun in her own solar system, the rest of us revolving like planets in orbit around her."

She laughed. "I like that image. You pretty much nailed it."

"Well, yeah, but sweetie, I don't want to be just another little planet under her sway. We need to have our own solar system. I mean, I've grown up hearing all these mother-in-law jokes and such, but this is shaping up into something absolutely ridiculous."

She bent forward and gently tweaked his left cheek. "You, my beloved, are the owl master. Now and forever. After we are married, I will go where you go and do what you say, and Ma will never come between us. Whenever I have to choose between the two of you, and I will, the choice will always be you. *Always.*"

That's a relief.

The phone rang.

She answered. "Oh, hi, Ma! How are you? Are you going to get here in time for the wedding?"

Brad could hear the replies just as clearly as if he were holding the phone next to his ear.

"Honeychiles, I already tol' you that you daddy's spirit promised I'd be there jes in time. He never can tell no lie. He's a watchin' you from de heavens as we speak. He know all dat about ta happen."

"Ma, this is getting crazier than usual, even for you. Daddy got here days ago, and he's sitting in the living room right now relaxing and having a drink."

"Cherie, I no wanna talk 'bout dat Rougarou no more. I see it upset you and de bebs an' I no wanna do dat. Gots to take care de bebs. Keep your health up. Keep your spirits up. Be strong for dem bebs. Be strong for the trial 'bout to come you way. Do-na worry, cherie, your new man, your outlaw, and de good Rougarou will save you. But I still worry about de bebs. Your daddy spirit won't tell me in my dreems how de bebs make it in you trial."

Worry crossed Mary Lou's face. "Ma, where are you right now?"

"I do-na know."

"Why did you call, then, Ma?"

"To tell you I loose Billy Bupp in Toccoa. Don' worry 'bout him ruinin' you weddin'."

"Toccoa? You're going the wrong way, Ma! That's further away than you were in Richmond last week!"

"Bah, Reesh-mon. She full of sheets. Had to go back ta get rid de Billy Bupp. T'ain't easy shedding him when he no wanta be shed."

"Where's Crazy Joe?"

"He in jail. Don' worry 'bout him ruinin' you weddeen neither."

"In jail? Where?"

"Someplace in Carolina."

"North or South? Where exactly?"

"Honeychile, you know I hardly ever remember nothin' exactly. Don' axe question lak dat."

"Shouldn't we bail Crazy Joe out?"

"Not till aftah da weddeen. I find him again when eet safe."

"Why is he in jail anyway? What did he do?"

"Helps himself ta ever-theen in liquor store. Crazy Joe go crazy in Carolina super store. Saw a sign by tha carts sayin' hep yo-self and thought it was a day for free pickins. Never seens so much whiskey, wine, beer, stuff lak dat. Jes take all he could carry, but de po-leece no lak dat and stop 'im."

"Anything else, Ma?"

"Non, cherie. I needs to get away anyhows. I do a Crazy Joe kinda t'ing, too, and de alarm still goin' off. Gots to get away. Hear de siren a'comin'?"

Good grief!

"Bye, Ma…see ya—you—tomorrow." She hung up.

"So who are Crazy Joe and Bill Bupp, anyway?" Brad asked.

"Those are my cousins, the craziest bad-ass twins ever seen in Cajun territory—maybe the whole wide world!"

"What is that supposed to mean?"

"They've always been very protective of me while I was growing up. That is, when they weren't almost killing me with their stupid practical jokes."

I can't stand that term! A joke should be funny. How can it be practical when it hurts the victim and only the bully thinks it is funny? "So if they were protective of you most of the time, how bad could their practical jokes get?"

"You don't want to know! One time in third grade, I think it was our first day at St. Martinville Primary School, Billy Bupp held me up in the air, and Crazy Joe pulled my panties right off!"

Something about that image stimulated two different, incompatible parts of Brad's psyche. He felt a stirring deep in his loins, but his fists also clenched with rage—fists that in his mind's eye he could see pulverizing two eight-year-old bullies.

She continued, a sour look on her face. "Kept his eyes closed, of course, or I would have scratched 'em out! And he knew that! He just wanted my panties to play a trick on the teacher. Put 'em on the teach's chair when he wasn't looking and made the whole class—'cept me—roar with laughter when he tried to sit down, saw those dainty white drawers, lifted them up with his pointer stick, and dropped 'em into the trash.

"I was embarrassed half to death. The rest of that day if either of them boys tried to talk to me, I punched him right in the nose. Crazy Joe got home bloody *that* day!"

"After stuff like that they were still protective of you? Sounds like you didn't need much protection!"

"Never said I did. I was a Cajun girl. I knew how to look after myself. But they took it upon themselves to harass and destroy any boy who ever showed any kind of interest in me at all."

"You're talking about teenage dating, that kind of thing?"

"Sure, that. I had my first date when I was fifteen, and Crazy Joe and Billy Bupp saw him kiss me goodnight at the end, and after I was inside, they grabbed him, tied him up, and hauled him out by pirogue to a little island in the bayou and left him there overnight! Poor guy was scared to death the gators would eat him while he slept and climbed as high as he could into a large bush, there being no trees on that island. He was scratched up something awful by the time his parents and I found him the next dawn. After that I couldn't get a boy brave enough to ask me out on a date until I was in college!

"But even before dating at the age where I mostly hated boys and didn't want anything to do with them anyway, they would go after any preteen boy who talked to me or looked at me a certain way. You ever play marbles as a young boy?"

"Marbles? Not really. I got a small set for a birthday, age nine or ten, I guess. But I never got into any competitive games or anything. Just played with them a few times at home, learned how to use the shooter to ricochet one of the littler ones around the room. That kind of thing."

"Well, marbles was a big thing for boys that age in Cajun country in those days. At recess they'd draw a huge circle in the dust, put up their marbles bets essentially—I later used to call it Cajun roulette—and try to shoot each other's marbles out of the circle. If you got one, you could keep it."

"Sounds harmless enough. A good way to learn eye-hand coordination before the advent of video games."

"Harmless, huh? You ever hear of razoo?"

"Razoo? Can't say that I have."

"Well, at some point in the game, usually about the time the bell signaled the end of recess, one of the boys would yell 'Razoo!' and there'd be a mad free-for-all as all the boys would grab all the marbles they could and try to keep hold of 'em."

"Well, boys will be boys. I did my share of rough and tumble as a lad. And it's not as if they were stealing money. I mean, even to a poor kid a couple of marbles isn't worth much. You could buy a bag full for under a dollar in those days."

"Brad, remember when I told you that Cajuns like to be subtle and indirect?"

"Of course. Many times."

"Brad, those boys would grab for *all* your marbles if they saw you talking to me in a friendly way."

"So?"

"Geez, you still don't get it? I guess you dry-landers would call the extra marbles family jewels. Comprendre vous now?"

Brad involuntarily winced and squeezed his legs together. "Well, they couldn't actually steal those, now, could they?"

"They'd sure try. They'd hang on and squeeze until you cried and yelled uncle. Or until some teacher popped over and caught them up the side of the head with a fist."

"Well, I can certainly see that they were rough-n-tough kids. But didn't they grow up and mature a little bit by now?"

"Brad, have you ever heard of *chivaree*?"

"Sure, mostly from reading history and old literature. When a couple would get married, the townsfolks had license to play pranks on them like standing outside the house on the wedding night, mingling about holding torches, and chanting till the bride's mother would bring out a sheet with maidenhead blood on it.

"But that kind of crap died out a century ago, right? The tradition survives now with people just tying cans to the honeymooners' rear bumper and using whitewash to write silly things like just married on the windshield. Right?"

"Brad, no tradition ever dies out in Cajun land. In fact, they added to it. The Cajun mob doesn't just chant and mill about, they beat on pots and pans and ring bells and make every noise they can, a right raucus tintamarre, until the groom or one of the bride's family emerges, and everyone cheers."

"So you mean to say that Crazy Joe and Billy Bupp intended some more primal and ferocious chivaree for *us*? That's why Ma has been trying to ensure they never made it up here?"

"You got it. I don't know exactly what they had planned. But as soon as we announced our engagement, those boys went all over St. Martinville bragging about all the chivaree they would do. It would be the biggest and baddest anyone from that parish had ever seen! That's the main reason Ma and I decided to have the wedding up here."

Just then Dad walked in. "Did I hear you two talking about chivaree?"

"Yes, Dad."

"Hoo-ee! I remember the chivaree that my father-in-law pulled when I married up with Josephine. But that was nuttin' compared to what ol' Crazy Joe and Billy Bupp been doing all these years."

Brad interrupted. "Sounds to me as if both twins are equally crazy. Why don't you call the other Crazy Billy?"

"No," said Dad. "They both be equally wild and fierce. But Joe, he jus' plan crazy! Why once when he was about fifteen, he was barefoot 'n fishin' down de bayou. A midsize gator snuck up and bit a chunk right out of his right foot. Gotta couple of toes and a good piece of the ball, too."

"Yuck!" interrupted Brad.

"That Joe, he didn't cry or run away or anythin' like what a teen up here would be like ta do. He jes' kep screamin' curses at that gator, grabbed his snout tight shut with both hands, flipped him over, and drowned him right then 'n there, right in de bayou.

"That gator put up a heckuva fight, scratching Joe's arms till blood filled the water. That leather tail thrashed and kicked, and the scales scarred Joe's back, but he didna let go! Coupla big gators in dem parts heard the ruckus and smelt the blood and slithered over to help their youngun or finish Joe or something.

"By that time, the youngun was daid. Joe stood there in the water and lifted up the carcass with both hands high overhead and dared the big 'uns to come get another piece of him. Screamed out he would do the same to any gator, large or small, whoever came near him again. T'other gators swam off, scared out o' they wits."

Mary Lou broke in. "Ever since that day, people called him Crazy Joe. Brad, that story is mostly true, not just more of Dad's Cajun BS. After Joe got the dead gator up on the bank, he tore open his jaws, got the chunk of his foot out, and tried to sew it back on himself."

"You're kidding."

"Nope. Of course it didn't work, and by the time they got him to the hospital, it was too late to re-attach it. Crazy Joe has walked with a limp ever since."

Dad's face looked annoyed. "What do you mean by Dad's Cajun BS? I always tell the truth, leastwise how it feels ta me."

Mary Lou reached over and gave him a hug. "I didn't mean to hurt your feelings, Daddy. It's just that the rest of the world doesn't always *feel* the truth the same way you do."

"You mean to tell me that Crazy Joe and Billy Bupp don' do the biggest, baddest chivaree in the whole world?"

"Well, I'm with you there, Daddy, if by that you mean the whole world we know."

"Why dem boys kidnapped the priest just before the Alphonse Babineaux wedding and brought a jackass inta church to take his place! *After* filling his face with two boxes of ex-lax!"

Mary Lou nodded at Brad in confirmation.

"Why Alphonse and Adelaide had to find da priest tied up in de graveyard 'hind the church and do the weddin' dere! Then hightail it out de whole parish so they's could have a honeymoon wit'out dem boys tryin' ta crawl inda windows all nite!

"Why dem boys set fire to de justice o' da peace's house for the Gaudet weddin' and nearly kilt the whole weddin' party! Den dey trew firecrackers and M-80s at the fire people comin' ta help *and* at the weddin' peoples trying to escape. 'Bout blowed off de judge's little finger whilst he was holdin' up de good book!"

Mary Lou kept nodding.

Brad asked, "You mean they actually tried to burn the wedding party alive?"

"Oh, no!" she exclaimed. "Chivaree that rough might occasionally result in a death, but that's not the intent. Those boys didn't try to set the house on fire. They sneaked into the cloak room to set off fireworks during the ceremony and set the heavy winter coats on fire by accident."

Dad continued, looking very amused by his recol-
lections. "Why dem boys swept de whol' party of de
Thibadeaux weddin' up inna little bag, tied it ta balloon,
and tossed it up ovah da ol' oak tree on town square.
Couldn't had that weddin' atall 'cepting Granma Moses
grabbed her double barrel shotgun 'n popped dat balloon
so's they could have da weddin' in ta top branches dat ol'
tree!"

Mary Lou shook her head and grimaced.

"Why dem boys tried to toss the next weddin' party—
the Broussards—rite inta outer space so Grandma, she
couldn't rescue dem no mo'—"

"Dad," broke in Brad. "I need to get back to work.
Would you mind joining me in my study?"

Wedding Minus Twenty-Six Hours

In his eBay war room, Brad took a seat at his desk and offered Dad the other chair there.

"Dad, I saw that brown patch in the front yard when I got home. Did you do that?"

"No, son. That happened last night while we were asleep. I heard a loud noise like fireworks but just one. I had your .357 with me under the pillow, and I lay awake a long time listening to see if anything else would happen. You know, something like people breaking in. But that was it. After a while I got up and sneaked around, peering out all the windows and looking for anything else out of the ordinary, but that was all. In the next day's light I looked around and saw that patch but couldn't figure out what it was."

"I don't think it was fireworks."

"Agreed, now that I've seen it. That's what it reminded me of when it went off, but there was no sign of a burnt-out bottle rocket or tufts of gunpowder-stained paper or anything else like you would expect from that."

"Dad, did you ever use hand grenades in the guard?"

"Of course, during training."

"You think it could have been that?"

"Maybe, or perhaps some other kind of military ordnance like that. But I didn't see any stray pieces of metal either."

"Any pieces might have scattered under the snow."

"So, Brad, you think maybe this has something to do with our eBay case, the high bidder maybe wanting to scare us off that radioactive hand auction?"

"That's my best guess, Dad, until we get further evidence pointing to anything else. Though I still find it puzzling. If they were going to go to that much trouble, why stop there? Wouldn't they throw a brick through the window with a threatening note on it or something?"

"There was a note the next morning."

"Why didn't you tell me?"

"I never got to read it. When I opened the door, a note fell out of the crack. But before I could pick it up, the wind blew it away. Cold winter wind this morning. I chased after it a bit, but it flew clean out of sight, and I lost track of it. Sorry."

"Not your fault. You had no way to know the note was even there until it was too late. I think it is safe to assume it was some kind of threat associated with the explosion to prove they meant business. Still, it would have been nice to see it, maybe pick up a clue or two."

Dad pursed his lips. "You seem to have a lot of trouble swirling around you, son."

"Yeah, sure seems that way. I guess once you stand up to one of these creeps, all the other vermin slip out of the cracks and come at you, too."

"Yeah."

"By the way, Dad. With all this other stuff going on and my sudden trip overseas, I never got to ask you what you found out when you went to all the hardware and sheet metal stores asking about lead coffins and the like."

"Not much, really, but I got to tell you, it was fun checking it out. I'd go into the store, find the manager, and go into my Cajun routine. They would act like they thought I was Borat the Second coming from a different country this time. You could see it in their eyes…in their expression. There would be a little display of shock or dismay at first, but then they'd try to control that. Then concern that this poor idiot was running around loose. Finally concern with how the heck they could get rid of me. It was all I could do to keep from laughing!"

Brad did chuckle. "Can you give me an example? Walk me through one of these interviews, please."

"Sure. I'd go up and say, 'You be de manager?' and they'd nod.

"I'd say, 'I'm new to dese parts, and my boss needs somepin, and if you alls can't hep me, I might get fired! Can you hep?' and they'd look uncomfortable but say something like 'Sure, if I can. What's the problem?'

"Then I'd say, 'My boss ordered a load of lead sheets and a lead box or coffin kinda thing. But he forgets to give me de name o' de store! Was it you'se? Had to be in the last few days.' Then I'd do something stupid like pick my teeth with a fingernail while they stopped to think or check the records."

Brad slapped his thigh and laughed. "That is so cool, Dad. I never would have thought to handle it just like that."

"So they'd come back and say something like, 'Sorry... uh...sir. Nothing like that here this week. Have you tried Bailey's down the way?' I'd thank them profusely and try to shake their hand with the one of mine just barely out of my mouth.

"That's when I liked to die laughing, watching them shrink back like I had offered them skunk roadkill on a plate."

"So were you able to pull that at all the stores I gave you on the list?"

"All eleven-teen of them."

"And all the responses were negative?"

"All except at Bailey's. Three of the guys I talked to mentioned Bailey's, but I got there last. And they confirmed it. A lead box was sold to"—Dad pulled a sheet of folded paper out of his pocket "—a Raymond Pincer over on Rosemont Avenue in Frederick."

"Dad, what do you say you and I run over and pay Mr. Pincer a visit?"

"Sure, but what about Mary Lou?"

"Is she really as good a shot as you let on the other day? I don't mean all the hyperbole, but you really taught her to shoot, and she can handle the more powerful firearms?"

"Well, of course I was joshing about some of the targets. But that girl could shoot full sized twelve-gauge shotguns, .30-06 rifles, and magnum revolvers by the time she was a teenager. Killed lots of gators with that high-powered stuff when she'd be out on the bayous collecting wild rice and hunting and such."

Brad shook his head slowly and thought back to when he had given her the relatively low-power .380 pistol and she pretended to "let" him teach her how to shoot. *That must be what passes for feminine wiles among Cajun girls…at least those transplanted to foreign territory.* "That little rascal! She let me think she knew next to nothing and I was helping her turn into such a good shot."

"Well, Brad, you gotta realize that Cajun girls are always looking to care for their menfolk, whether it's in the bedroom, the kitchen, or the thinking room." Dad pointed at his own noggin. "They know no browbeat, torn-down, dispirited fellow will be much good to them."

Brad clicked his tongue. "Not sure what to think about that, Dad. But I'll ponder on it a while. Meanwhile, why don't we leave her both handguns, lots of ammo, and a jury-rigged safe room just in case. Ma's been warning of some trouble ahead, and that explosion and note has me concerned, too, although if that was from the eBay bidder and you did cooperate by dropping out of the auction, it doesn't seem too likely he will come back."

"True, I gave him what he wanted, so why not drop it? Now, Ma, on the other hand, oftentimes gets these feelings about the future. Usually she says it's her garden windchimes telling her what's going to happen."

"And does it ever come true?"

"Well, sure, sometimes. You know what they say about a stopped clock?"

"Of course."

"Now on the other hand, she seems to have convinced herself that I died on the plane coming up here and that my spirit is giving her messages in her dreams. She's never pulled that one before, so I wouldn't put too much stock on vague warnings based on that. I mean, look here, she was scared to death I wouldn't make it by air, but I did! See what I mean?"

They both went upstairs and carried out Brad's plan.

Mary Lou seemed amused. "Brad, we're supposed to get married in less than twenty-four hours, and you two plan to go out gallivanting around some more?"

"We won't leave Frederick County—I promise. We should be back soon. Dad's just helping me with one of my army projects, and after that explosion in the yard last night, we don't want to leave you alone and unprotected."

"Shoot. I'm Cajun. I'm never unprotected. If I can handle Crazy Joe and Billy Bupp, I can handle most anything."

"Sure, of course you can. But don't forget the twins. You're not as quick on your feet as usual. You can't afford to get too stressed out. Any bad guys come around here, you just get behind these barricades we set up in the back bathroom, call the sheriff, call us on the cell, and we'll come a running back. You could hold off an Indian attack with all these guns and ammo until we get here."

"Sure, if it makes you feel better. But what can possibly go wrong?"

Oh, no, not another invocation of the law of opposites! We must have a doozy headed our way.

Wedding Minus Twenty-Three Hours

Brad and Dad arrived at the Raymond Pincer place on Rosemont Avenue, a nice little rancher not far from Fort Detrick's back gate. There was no car in the driveway, but Brad couldn't see into the closed garage. There could be something there.

Brad rang the doorbell. No answer. He rang again and then knocked. Nothing.

"Brad, you ever get arrested for a B and E?"

"Can't say as I have. And I don't care for breaking and entering now unless we've got more evidence than just suspicion."

Just then the garage door opened. A large man, maybe about twenty-five, headed toward a Mercury Coupe in the interior.

"Mr. Pincer?" asked Brad.

"Nope, he's my roommate, but he's not here right now."

"Do you know where he is?"

"Nope."

"Any idea how I can reach him?"

"You're out of luck, friend."

"Mind if I ask you a few questions?"

"You've just been asking me a few questions practically all morning. Why don't you just mosey along and leave me to my business?"

Brad would not be deterred. "You know anything about a heavy lead box?"

The man transformed into a tower of rage and stormed toward them. Shoulders back, fists tight, whole body stiff like he was about to dead lift several hundred pounds. "I told you to get lost! And you can forget about any lead box. Just shut your mouth about that, or I'll teach you a lesson you'll never forget!" He paused, right next to his garbage can about ten feet from them.

Brad pulled out his wallet and flipped it open for half a second as if to show him something inside. "That's not how it works in this city, son. I'm Detective Wallis, and this here is Detective Burns, and we have a warrant for your arrest."

The man picked up the garbage can and threw it at them then darted to his coupe and sped away, screeching tire marks into the driveway pavement as he fled.

Brad and Dad easily dodged the can, but it delayed them a second from getting to the car in time to grab the man. They stood there, the acrid smell of burning tire rubber filling their noses. *Should we pursue?*

"What would you say to a B and E *now?*" asked Dad.

That's a better idea. While he still had it in his memory, Brad wrote down the Mercury's model type and license tag number. "Just don't touch anything, Dad. Don't leave any fingerprints."

"Got it."

X

It turned out they didn't even need to break anything to enter. The back of the open garage was filled with metal working tools. A heavy duty work table, a vise, some sheets of lead, a soldering iron, and lots of lead solder all about— not just the spools, but drops that had been melted then fell to the table and re-hardened there.

Then Brad spied it in a separate table in the workroom behind the garage. He had to open that door, but it wasn't locked. He shielded his hand with his jacket then grabbed the handle through the cloth and opened it.

Inside was a writing table with maps and diagrams all about.

"Come look at this, Dad."

They saw diagrams for making lead containers of different sizes, including smaller ones that would fit inside larger ones. They saw an instruction sheet on how to add a lead coating to Kevlar heavy duty work gloves to make them protective against radiation as well as intense heat. Then *it*.

A sketched out, hand-made map in black ink on a plain sheet of paper. The only writing for a legend of any kind was hand-lettered along the top: Catoctin. In the middle was a sort of rectangular area with buildings and sites mapped out, looking much like a Boy or Girl Scout camp. One of the largest squares in that circle had an X marked in the middle, and it had the only other printed label on the page.

"Aspen."

"What's this mean, son?"

"Well, the Catoctin Mountains are those ones you've seen just a mile or so west of Frederick. They run along a north-south ridge, which connects from here up to near Thurmont, close to the Pennsylvania border. Up where Camp David is."

Dad whistled and shook his head.

"And Aspen…well, that's where the president stays when he's up there. His private quarters."

✕

Brad tried to call Deputy Lancer of the Frederick County Sheriff's office, but the man wasn't in. He left a phone message.

"Deputy Lancer? This is Major Brad Stout. Remember this morning when you said you would love to help if I came across an incident like that one last fall? Well, here is your chance." He proceeded to give the name and address of Raymond Pincer, the car model and license tag of the unknown perp, and left a few hints of what might be found in the garage and workroom. He described his suspicion that there was one or more inside men at Camp David working with these presumed terrorists. At the last, he mentioned the suspected hand grenade attack at his house and asked the deputy to see if he could arrange more patrols in that area until Brad's return.

Then Brad turned to Dad. "We've got to get into Camp David and warn the president. Otherwise, I think he's going to go to sleep tonight atop a monstrous radioactive source, and he's never going to wake up the next morning."

"Can't you call someone to take care of it?"

"My only point of contact in the White House is already at Camp David himself, and he warned me that his phone line at the office has been shut down by now. I don't have a number where I can reach him!"

"Then let's get a move on, son. Let's fly like a heron and land like a bullfrog...*croak*."

Brad thought the sound was so deep and throaty that it came from a real amphibian. He dashed through a yellow light, careened around a corner, and floored it.

They reached Highway 15 and sped north toward Thurmont.

$$\times$$

"I can get us in," said Dad. "Back home, nearly all my life I've been able to sniff out traps, alarms, Crazy Joe type pranks, and everything like that. I can sense 'em. Just see it in my head. My guard commander said I'd make the perfect point man in 'Nam, but it never came to that. Remember in *Southern Comfort* all the booby traps and surprises the Cajuns had for the guardsmen and used to take them out one at a time? I knew all that kinda stuff. You wouldn't catch me stepping into a snare or triggering a Louisiana black bear trap.

"I can just see 'em. Have some kind of sixth sense. I can get us in. May not be able to get us back out, but I can get us in."

"We'll worry about getting out when the time comes. The important thing is to get in and save the president's life."

"It's worth the risk. I agree with you. Not sure Mary Lou would, though. I see us missing the wedding over this."

Brad grimaced and nodded. "Think she'll ever be able to forgive me, Dad? Us?"

"Oo ye yi! Cajun women sure know how to rage, I can tell you that. They're the real ragin' Cajuns. But eventually the love in their hearts will overcome it…as long as they know you had a worthy reason for what you done. Now, on the other hand, don't you never mess around on my little girl. No Cajun woman ever forgive her man for something like that. That's just selfish. No excuse for that."

"Dad, I'm Mary Lou's for life. I want you to know that. There'll never be any messing around on her—you can count on that."

"Let's do this thing, then."

"First, let me fill you in on what we're up against so you can program your sixth sense to pick it out. The news media always just refers to Camp David as a presidential retreat, which is true, but that's not all it is. It's actually a military base—a navy base, of all things, on a mountain top rather than near water, officially called the Naval Support Facility Thurmont. And it is the most secure residence in the entire world except for the White House."

"Naturally."

"Dad, I've lived in this area all my life, and I know just about as much about the place as you can know without actually being there. I even have a map of the place from the old days before security got so tight. It shows the walking trails, the president's lodge, the cabins for other staff and visiting dignitaries, the incredible swimming pool, tennis courts, golf area, and so on. They even have an area for shooting skeet. About a hundred and twenty-five acres overall."

"Sounds like my kind of place! I love hunting camps!"

"It's getting into that area that will be the problem. Now, beyond the outer perimeter of Camp David are some wonderful public areas every bit as beautiful as the interior of the presidential retreat. I'm talking about the nature scenes themselves, not the luxurious amenities the president enjoys. Anybody can freely wander around the Catoctin Mountain Park and see the trees, cliffs, lake, streams, waterfalls, and so on. It's the most beautiful area in this region."

"Let's go see it!"

"Now let me tell you about the security zones between the public area and the interior of the private area. There are three main areas of security, delineated by three concentric fences. The outer fence, the one the public can see, is still considered a pretty friendly zone. As long as you don't try to cross that fence, you probably won't be arrested. In the area surrounding that fence you see friendly type signs like for national parks, showing where to make food deliveries and so forth. If you come at the fence in the wooded areas, there are signs warning you to go back, but they are still pretty polite.

"Over the years I've had lots of friends wander into that area by accident. Just make the wrong turn leaving the waterfall, for instance, and if you leave the trail at just the wrong point, you may not notice the signs right away. In an instant a guard will suddenly appear from nowhere and politely ask you to reverse direction. That happens all the time, totally unintentionally by most tourists.

"And once in a while, some idiot tourist may try to be funny on purpose to see how far he can get. The guards can tell whether it was by accident or someone being a smart aleck, but as long as you don't argue and do obey their warning to leave the area, you won't get into trouble. There are sound detectors in the trees, and they'll record any of your conversation. They'll know if you were just chasing after your dog or telling your companion, 'Hey, Bubba, watch this.'"

"I can get us through that, no problem. Won't matter if the guard or his post is in camouflage—I can see right through all of that."

"Yes, but that's the easy part. The outer fence is electrified—not to a dangerous level to kill anyone, but just so they can detect if someone touches it or tries to cut it."

"It's not a high wall, right? Just a fence?"

"Well. I've never seen it myself, but my friends who have describe it that way."

"I can get us over that. What's next?"

"The tertiary security zone lies between that outer fence and the next fence. Anybody caught wandering around in there will definitely get arrested, as the signs throughout that area warn. You'll be detained and questioned and booked, but you might be able to talk your way out of it if you can come up with a plausible reason for violating the law. You won't necessarily go to court and end up with a long prison sentence. They'll apprehend and detain you, but they won't shoot on sight as long as you obey their commands—you know, lie down on your stomach, put your hands behind your back...all that arrest stuff."

"They must have even more sensors in this area, right?"

"Oh, yeah. It's not just the guards on patrol. They've got cameras in the trees, motion detectors, pressure detectors, vibration detectors, sound detectors, and police dogs trained to sniff out a human hair at a hundred yards."

"But those detectors have to be calibrated so they don't go off every time a pine cone falls or a rabbit hops, right? There must be a sensitivity cut-off at a certain threshold."

"Of course," said Brad, "But I'm not sure what the threshold is."

"I can get us through that."

"Dad, you're not just flinging Cajun BS again, are you? You know, that stuff about swallowing rivers and spitting out bayous and stuff?"

"No, son, I'm not. All my years in the bayou there was no Cajun good as I was at escaping detection by rattle-snakes and gators, avoiding swamp spider webs, and so on. Once I was just drifting in my pirogue near the bank under some low-lying branches of the trees, and I just *knew* there was a snake in a branch ahead planning to slither off and land in my boat. I could just read his mind. At the last second, I just willed my boat to veer a couple of inches to the right, and that ol' snake just plopped into the water instead."

"Okay, well if we get through that zone, then we've got to cross the second fence. Not just barbed wire but razor wire. You can actually kill yourself if you get stuck in the middle of that. You'd be begging the guards to come cut you loose and take you away to a prison infirmary."

"No problem."

"You're sure you're not BSing me? One wrong move, and neither of us will ever see Ma or Mary Lou again."

"I swear. As long as it's not over ten feet tall."

"I'm not sure. The next zone is the secondary security zone. There are explosive mines here, ones they can trigger electronically from the security control room. When the field is on, each mine is pressure and vibration sensitive. You step on it, *boom*! You vibrate the ground near it, *boom*! You set one off, and the man in the control room watching the video camera feed can push a button and set off the whole cluster of mines around you."

"I handled live mines in the guard. I could find and disable planted ones with my Gerber Mark II knife."

"That's good, Dad, but these mines are way more advanced than the ones from your day. A flip of the control switch, and they can turn the whole field off while they send a team out to collect your scattered body parts."

"Don't worry. That won't happen to us."

"And there are guards patrolling through there in an un-mined path only they know the extent of. It's shoot on sight here. No warnings, no arrests. Just a sudden bullet in the head, and then it's lights out. Forever. And, Dad, I've got to tell you, these aren't mall cops and private night guards and stuff. These are marines. And they are from the toughest, most elite unit in the whole corps.

"Every one of them belongs to the MSC-CD, the Marine Security Company, Camp David. Each is hand picked, extensively tested, and very highly trained. Each one must undergo the most thorough security check provided by the DOD and must attain the highest level of clearance in the military, Yankee White."

"US marines? I could probably get us through there if I used you as a decoy and took one or two of the guards out. But I'm not about to hurt a US Marine, not even for the president. One's just as valuable as the other, as far as I'm concerned."

Brad shrugged. "You're right. I'm sure any of them would freely give his life to protect the president. But I sure wouldn't take it from him to protect the president when the grunt is just doing his job."

Dad continued. "What were you saying a while ago about a food delivery entrance?"

Wedding Minus Twenty Hours

Brad stopped his car right after turning off Highway 15, west onto Route 77, the mountain approach road.

"Dad, I can only see two possibilities here, and I'm not sure which is best."

"Talk 'em out, and we'll figure it out together."

"I've seen the food delivery and service gate many times. You can get pretty close to that without attracting any trouble. At that point you'd never even know it was Camp David. It looks just like anything else in the park, except it is marked private."

"Sure, they're trying to be friendly like, just the same as at the fence separating the public and private areas that you were talking about."

"Overhead along the gate I noticed radiation detectors, chemical agent detectors, and biological detectors. They're structured and painted to blend in with the rough woodwork of the rustic gate. Most people would never notice them, but I work with all that stuff, so I know."

"How do you reckon the terrorists will get the radioactive material through all that?"

"That's where those multiple layers of lead boxes come in. It's kind of like those Russian nesting dolls where you open the biggest one, and inside is another. You open that, and inside is a smaller one, and so on. One regular lead box alone would block most of your radiation, but it would allow enough through to set off the detectors."

"And if you had one giant box with several inches of lead, it would be too heavy to cart anywhere."

"Exactly. So I figure those two guys must have a delivery driver working with them. They set down the biggest box first, lay the next one inside that, and so on. Finally they took the smallest box, the one holding the radioactive hand of death, and put that one in last. Then they closed all the lids."

"Well that gets them through the radiation detector," concluded Dad, "But when they inspect the goods, won't the guards be suspicious about an enormous lead box?"

"Precisely. They must have some way to disguise it. Maybe build it into the base of their van or hide it in the middle of a crate of hams or something. I can't quite visualize anything they could do that would be foolproof. They'd be taking a big risk."

"Well, those fellas that crashed into the World Trade Towers took a risk, didn't they? And those guys that attacked your AFRRI last year, right?"

"Point taken, Dad. As far as that goes, any wartime mission requires risk, and many fail, and many die. But the remaining warriors fight on."

"Well, we're never going to be able to guess how they hide it, but assuming it escapes detection, what other security do they—or we—have to cross through to get in at the service gate?"

"Well, for starters, you'd have to produce photo ID, and your names would have to be on the admit list kept with the guards. That's why I figure the terrorists must have one or more inside men on this. If you pass that, you go quite a distance on a normal-looking road until you reach the real security checkpoint, one out of sight from the public areas.

"That's where you'd run into armed guards with everything imaginable. They'd check your invoice and match it with the goods inside. They'd do an insta-check on your fingerprints. They'd search your vehicle for any kind of bombs. They'd pat you down for weapons. They'd swab various parts of the vehicle and your hands for gunpowder traces…all that kind of stuff.

"And if anything came out irregular, your vehicle wouldn't be going anywhere. Try to back up and escape, and your tires would instantly go flat on one of those sharp spike strips. Try to go forward, ditto. Plus with the push of a button at the guardhouse, massive steel barriers would shoot up from the ground in front and behind you."

"Brad, I can't get us through that."

"Of course not. And if you somehow could, the guards here have submachine guns with armor-piercing bullets."

"But what if nothing looked irregular, and you were allowed through to make your delivery? Then what?"

"You still would never see the inside of Camp David. You would proceed down a secure road a few hundred yards to the transfer dock where the Camp David staff would receive all your things and transfer them one at a time, after close inspection, to the other side of the platform where their own vehicles waited. That's why the bad guys have got to have an inside man or men. Someone to take the innermost lead box, the dangerous one, away with them into the safe zone."

"You figure someone who passed all those security checks would turn traitor?"

"Well, these guys aren't the elite marine corps guard group. These are navy specialists in the various fields, such as cooks and mess attendants, groundskeepers, maintenance men, and so on. They are specially selected and trained and naturally have to pass extensive background security checks, but it's not quite as tight as for the Marine Security Company guards. I'd hate to think one turned traitor on his own initiative, but one might have been blackmailed or otherwise extorted into helping."

"Oh, yeah," added Dad. "I remember in the Cold War how Soviet bombshell agents would throw some tail at a lonely American Embassy guard in Moscow or wherever then produce the pictures and threaten to expose him if he didn't work with them."

"Sad but true. It certainly didn't always work, but it caused a huge problem every time it did."

"So what are our two options?"

"We can try to commandeer the next delivery vehicle that runs through here, or we can just drive up to the service gate and try to talk our way in, explaining about the radiation plot and so on."

"Brad, I've always believed that honesty was the best policy."

"Good, Dad, thanks. My first thought was to try something more physical because of the time pressure, but now that we're here, I don't want to risk spilling any innocent blood…including our own. Let's go talk. I just hope we don't get hung up talking to no one important until after it is too late."

"Son, speaking of innocent blood…you realize we're probably going to miss the wedding. If we get inside, we can't just walk out when we're ready."

Brad looked glum.

Wedding Minus Nineteen Hours

At the outer delivery gate, the guard motioned Brad to stop. "Sir, I'm afraid you are going to have to turn around and get back to the main road. You are about to enter a secure zone, and you are not authorized to do so."

"I understand. I'll be perfectly willing to stay here and wait. But could you reach someone inside Camp David, preferably the chief of security, and let me speak with him or her from out here?"

A look of consternation crossed the guard's face. Likely he had to turn innocent tourists around just about every day of the week, but he probably hadn't heard Brad's request very often in his entire career. He made a hand signal to the other guards at the gate, and they suddenly looked twice as alert.

"Sir, I'm going to have to ask you to turn off your vehicle and step outside. Both of you. Give me the keys then please stand over there until we can sort this out."

Brad and Dad followed the instructions precisely. From nowhere, it seemed, two guards armed with submachine guns appeared and kept steady eyes on them. Meanwhile two others darted to the vehicle and made a thorough search, inside and out, using a mirror on a pole to check the undercarriage.

The first guard stepped over to Brad and asked for his ID. Ditto for Dad.

"Okay, Major Stout. Can you explain the reason for your request?"

"Certainly. I work at the Armed Forces Radiobiology Research Institute, and part of my job is tracking down radiological threats against the American government or its people. I have reason to suspect there is a radiological threat against the president of the United States at Camp David this very weekend. I would like to provide the details to your chief of security or whoever else he might designate."

"Sir, you have got to be kidding if you think we would allow a radiological device to pass through our security."

"I meant no offense. Quite possibly you will catch him on your own if he shows up. But I can help." *If he hadn't shown up already.*

"If I hadn't seen your military ID, sir, I would immediately dismiss you as a kook. We always get tons of those when the media announce in advance that the president will be here."

"I assure you I am not a kook. If you or someone else here call the AFRRI commander, he can fill you in on our previous progress in tracing this terrorist. We know of a very specific threat."

"Stay right where you are, and don't move a muscle. I'll check with my watch commander."

Moments later the guard returned. "Someone will be down shortly to speak with you. While you wait, you may rest on that bench if you like."

They did. It felt very cold sitting there in the open air, but the view was lovely. With all the leaves down for the winter, you could see through the trees up the hillside to the summit. The craggy rocks and ground were largely covered with snow, but it wasn't thick. Beautiful but not thick.

The minutes passed, and Brad kept glancing at his watch, feeling colder and colder. He could see his breath now in little clouds of condensation every time he breathed out. The two guards with submachine guns kept a close watch on them.

Finally a navy vehicle came down the mountain road behind the guard post, and a man in a navy uniform got out and walked toward them, his shoes crunching in the snow. He held out his hand and shook Brad's then Dad's.

"Major Stout, I'm sorry for the delay. I'm Lieutenant Commander Blume, the deputy chief of base security here. I've been trying to reach the AFRRI commander to verify your story but without success so far. I did reach the weekend staff duty officer, however, and he confirmed who you were and how you were the one who caught the dirty bomb terrorists last year…but not anything about a Camp David threat now."

"The SDO wouldn't know about that. That info has so far been restricted to the lab commander and the head of the radiation department, in addition to myself. I also taught my radiation defense course at the White

House last year to all the medical staff. Last week I called Commander Jefferson, the chief of the medical staff—he knows me personally—to inform him of a possible rad threat. But I didn't know many details at that point. I have much more specific information at this time."

"Hold on." Blume took the BR950 off his belt. "Blume here. Can you get me Commander Jefferson on the line?"

A moment later. "Jefferson here."

"Sir, this is Lieutenant Commander Blume. Can you tell me anything about a Major Brad Stout? He's here at the service gate to see you."

"Of course, he warned me about a possible rad threat this weekend at Camp David, and I passed the message along to the Secret Service."

"He says he has more specific information now."

"Can you bring him up to the perimeter guard post? I'll meet him and you there."

The three men and Blume's driver went up the winding road past the various checkpoints and fences, slaloming around the endless obstacles, and finally arrived at a rustic-looking guard post at the innermost fence from which Brad could see bits of the lodges and amenities beyond. His first glimpse of the interior of Camp David.

"Good to see you, Brad," said Dan Jefferson, shaking his hand. "Long time no see."

"Same here. Dan, this is my father-in-law, Pierre Boudreaux. Or soon to be. I'm scheduled to be married in a few hours."

Jefferson shook his hand, too. "So, Brad, I tried to call you back the other day, but you never answered."

"I was tied up with a sudden overseas mission…in Germany. Sorry about that."

"So what is the new information?"

"I know this is going to sound crazy. But we've been tracking an on-line sale of a radioactive source that is so potent that full body exposure of just fifteen minutes can kill a man."

Blume whistled. "Wow!"

Jefferson looked very serious. "You don't think—"

"My father-in-law and I have been trying to track down the buyer, and we think it is a Raymond Pincer who lives on Rosemont Avenue in Frederick. It could also be his partner. I don't know his name, but we got a good look at him and his vehicle and license tag. I reported all this in a phone message to Deputy Lancer in the Frederick County Sheriff's department a couple of hours ago. From maps and diagrams at the Pincer house, we concluded that they planned to deposit this deadly device somewhere in the Aspen Lodge."

"*Aspen!*" Jefferson exclaimed then hurriedly grabbed the desk phone. "Get me the head of the Secret Service detail here at David…*now!*"

Wedding Minus Seventeen Hours

Since Brad and Dad were the only eye-witnesses to one of the possible perps, the heads of Camp David security and the secret service detail both agreed, under the unusually extenuating circumstances, to admit the two men into the perimeter zone of the secure compound to help aid in the search. They had to empty their pockets of wallets, cell phones, keys, anything important, and leave them all behind. Blume was appointed as their escort and was ordered never to let them out of his sight.

Meanwhile, as a security precaution, they kept the president and the Middle East delegates away from Aspen Lodge and sent them into the bowels of the underground bomb shelter, dug deep into solid granite decades ago, deep enough to survive a direct nuclear attack on the scale possible in the 1960s.

All that afternoon and all the night long, Brad and Dad, the security people, and Commander Jefferson maintained a vigil in the security control room while teams of agents armed with radiac meters scoured every inch of the grounds and all the lodges and other buildings for any sign of radiation.

Nothing.

After a while, Dad asked Blume, "Say, did you ever see that film *Southern Comfort?*"

Blume stared wearily at Dad with glazed eyes. "Huh? What?"

✕

Wedding Minus Three Hours

It was six the next morning when Jefferson came back to see Brad. "Brad, we'd always rather be safe than sorry in the face of a credible threat. But we are picking up nothing radioactive. Just the normal background uranium readings from a granite mountain, but nothing higher than normal. I'm afraid to say, I think this is a false alarm."

"I don't know what to say. Everything pointed in this direction," said Brad.

"Your leads on the names you mentioned, the vehicle, and license tag also turned up nothing."

"Must have been a stolen vehicle. But the stuff at the house was confirmed, right?"

"Yes, of course. But there's no law against having a map of Camp David and some soldering materials in your workroom."

"I see."

"The president, frankly, is getting P-Oed and wants to get the peace conference back on track. All the major media from around the world are expecting an important announcement from Camp David at 0-8 hundred hours about progress toward peace in the Middle East."

"You're holding a press conference?" Brad's pulse began to accelerate.

"Yes."

"Where?"

"Well, it's traditional to hold it right in front of Aspen Lodge on that beautiful stone-paved walkway with the rustic-looking lodge behind."

"Has all the equipment been installed? The podium, all that stuff?"

"Well, normally it would have been done last night. But we held up everything to conduct the rad search. Oh, I get it…you're thinking the attack will come there. But we used radiacs to scan all that equipment, which was delivered yesterday shortly before you arrived and was all stacked up. Nothing. It is safe."

Safe inside its lead container maybe. But what if the installer opens it and the president stands right there for half an hour to an hour answering questions? He'd be dead tomorrow! "Do you mind if we watch before we leave?"

Dad broke in. "Son, we'd have to leave right now to make the wedding on time."

"I know, Dad, but I can see in my head that snake in the oak tree beside the bayou. I can read his mind. I know what he's going to do next."

"Son, you've got that look in your eye again. You know the one I mean. I'm with you, boy, all the way ta the end. Mary Lou will just have to wait."

✕

Wedding Minus One Hour

Brad watched as a team of men used dollies to transport the microphones, podium, and other transportation gear down to Aspen Lodge. Then Brad saw him.

"That's the man who tried to attack us at the terrorist safe house!" he shouted to his escort Lieutenant Commander Blume as he ran pell mell toward the man.

Dad followed just a step behind.

The man looked up, surprise all over his face, then recognition, then rage. He pulled from his vest pocket what looked to Brad like a ceramic knife, something which could evade metal detectors.

At full speed now, Brad leapt into the air and sent both feet into the man's chest, ignoring the deep slash sustained in his own left thigh from a stab of the knife.

The man collapsed on his back with an awful "Unghh!"

Dad leapt upon his right arm on the ground, and the man screamed. Dad tore the knife out of the perp's right hand and kicked it away.

Brad had landed on the turd's torso. Now he reached over and gave him a one-two punch to the jaw, a right and a left. He leapt up, ran to the podium, pulled back the little curtain, and there it was…a lead box about a foot square.

He kicked over the podium, leaving the lead box visible to all. Brad noted a spring latch on the lid, connected by wire to the mike controls. Probably turning on the mike would trigger the box to pop open automatically, just as the president was preparing to speak.

"Get your radiacs out again, please, and then open that box!"

✕

Wedding Minus Fifty Minutes

"Good Lord!" exclaimed Jefferson. "When they opened that box, their radiacs immediately pegged at fifteen hundred rads! That *would* have killed the president with just twelve to fifteen minutes of exposure! Thanks, Brad…and Mr. Boudreaux."

"May we leave now and have our cell phones back? I have the feeling my fiancée has called me eleven-teen times by now."

"Eleven-teen? You need some sleep, my friend. You don't know what you are saying anymore."

"Yeah, sleep to be sure. About thirty or forty hours sounds about right. But first we've got to get to the church. I'm scheduled to get married in about half an hour!"

"You'd better run along then, my friend. But give me a name and number to call so I can tell them you are on the way and where you've been. Otherwise they're liable to shoot you!"

✕

Wedding Minus Thirty-Two Minutes

As they walked toward Brad's car at the outer service gate, Dad turned to Brad and said, "We can still make it, Brad. We can get there in a wink, two fingersnaps, and three wags of a dog's tail."

Brad laughed. "Good one, Dad."

"I'm proud to add you to this family today, Brad! You really are an army of one."

Brad smiled and hugged his father with one arm around the waist as they raced to the car.

"An army of two, Dad! An army of two!"

Wedding Minus Fourteen Minutes

In the car racing down Highway 15 back toward Frederick, Dad said, "Brad, I hate to tell you, but you smell like road kill skunk that forgot his deodorant and that's been sitting flat in the sun for a couple of days. I'm sure I do, too. And your left leg is still bleeding. And we're wearing nothing but dirty shirts, jeans, and tennis shoes under our coats. Are you heading for the church like this?"

"Only way to make it, Dad. We can go home, get cleaned up, and dress up proper and then miss the whole thing. That don't make any sense."

"Dat true, son, too true."

"Dad, can you listen to all eleventeen of Mary Lou's messages on my cell phone for me? I'm actually rather scared to listen at his point. Plus, I'm driving."

"Sure." Dad took the cell and punched a few keys. "What's your password?"

"MLB2001."

"Of course! Mary Lou Boudreaux and the year you met. Nice. Hmm. Actually twenty-one messages, Brad. Not a good sign. A Cajun woman doesn't have that much to say when she's happy. She's just enjoying the moment.

But when she's upset, worried, or mad, she'll talk your ear off! You gotta watch out—I'm warning you!"

The minutes passed in near silence as Dad listened to one message after the other.

Racing as fast as he dared down the highway without risking a sure-fire speeding ticket, Brad glanced over now and then and saw the increasing consternation on his father-in-law's face. Once in a while Dad would pull the phone back from his ear a couple of inches, and Brad could hear screeching, but it seemed faint, as if Mary Lou were shouting from across the other side of a bayou.

Finally the tirade ended.

"Brad, I'm going to ask you a favor."

"Sure, Dad, anything."

"I don't want you to listen to these, and I don't want to tell you what she said. Let me just erase them all, okay?"

"But she's all right, isn't she? No bad guys came around while we were tied up at Camp David?"

"No, nothing like that. But here's the thing, son. Once she sets eyes on you at the church, all her worries and anger will vanish, and she'll forget she ever said those things in these calls. But, Brad, if you listen to them now, fifteen minutes before you see her all dressed in her beautiful wedding gown, you won't be able to forget. And I don't want to see you start your married life and your honeymoon thatta way."

Brad nodded. "I understand, Dad. Just erase 'em all."

He did so. "Good thinking, Brad. You know the key to happiness when living with a woman is knowing when to take seriously what she says and…when not to. They always know when they mean it or don't, but their men usually can't tell the difference."

"Dad, you know you are one of the wisest men I've ever known. I wish my own father had been more like you. I really do."

Dad smiled, reached over, and patted Brad on the back. "Thanks, son, that means a lot. Mary Lou told me about some of your troubles growing up. Children shouldn't have to grow up like that. And I know you won't be that way with Remy and Cindy Lou and whatever other chilluns you two kids cook up. I know you're a better man than that."

"Dad, I promised Mary Lou last fall when we barely escaped death in AFRRI's radiation rooms, and I'm promising you now, I will be the best father two Cajun twins ever had!"

Dad smiled. "I see a church! Is that the one?"

"Yup!"

Brad looked at his watch. Five minutes late! He stopped the car on the church lawn, and the two of them darted out. Even though both men had missed the planned wedding rehearsal of the evening before, Brad knew where to go from years of attendance.

Both of them took deep breaths, knowing the wedding attenders would all be shocked at their appearance. Brad pointed out the room where the bride should be so Dad could join his daughter for the processional, started to dash toward his own place in the front, took one glance into the sanctuary, then nearly passed out.

36

Brad went limping back toward the bridal waiting room. "Dad! Hold up!"

The older man had his hand on the door but froze. "What's the matter, son? Is no one there? I saw plenty of cars out front."

"No, that's not it. I just saw the most beautiful woman over thirty that I've ever seen in my entire life."

"Oh, that's probably Ma. So she did make it in time!"

"There's something else, Dad. She looks too young to be anything more than Mary Lou's big sister!"

"Well she was only fourteen when we married. Her pop said she had to wait till then. That's the real reason he didn't cotton to me at first, Brad. I sorta kinda left that part out when I told you my life story earlier. Then Mary Lou came along right after Ma turned fifteen."

"Dad, there's something else!"

"What? Don't tell me Billy Bupp made it!"

"No...it's about the gorgeous woman. She's hand-cuffed to a police woman who's sitting right next to her."

"Well, that's for sure Ma, then. Brad, this is sounding more and more like *my* wedding!"

Brad darted down the narthex to the south transept door, hesitantly opened it, wished his sister could be here for this, and took his place at the front of the sanctuary. There stood his best man, Lieutenant Commander Sam Brubake, in his finest navy dress white uniform, looking proud as a young man bringing home his first regular paycheck. Brad, looking and smelling like two-day old dead skunk took his place next to Sam, who only smiled at him, not saying a word. Catching glimpses of the small crowd behind them, he noted several of his army and air force work friends in their finest dress uniforms as well.

Brad would never live this day down. He would be *the* joke at AFRRI until the place closed…in a couple of hundred years.

The base chaplain took his place in front of them and began. "Ladies and gentlemen, this is highly irregular, but as officiator at this solemn ceremony, I feel it is my duty to point out to those who may not have seen the news this morning—"

He took a deep breath, looked toward Brad and nodded, then looked toward the back where Brad assumed Mary Lou was holding her father's arm by now, and nodded again.

"That there is a very good reason that the groom and the bride's father are not dressed in more customary attire for a wedding. Their every moment for the past twenty-four hours has been absorbed up at Camp David saving the life of the president of these United States and helping to keep the Middle East peace process on track. Ladies and gentlemen, I ask you to give these two gentlemen a hand before we proceed with the ceremony!"

Everyone clapped vigorously. Some cheered. Some gave a standing ovation. Brad looked over at Ma, and she was whistling with two fingers in her mouth and alternating that with what Brad took as war cries. If Andrew Jackson's Cajuns had sounded like that back in 1815, no wonder the British never came back!

Brad looked over at Dad and Mary Lou at the rear of the sanctuary. Dad still looked like two-day dead skunk, too, but he had a proud grip on his daughter and stood at full attention till the applause subsided.

Mary Lou smiled and mouthed something silently in Brad's direction, but he couldn't read her lips from that distance.

Then Wagner's bridal chorus resounded from the pipe organ, and the two of them began to march down the aisle.

Brad watched her glide toward him, and the hopes and dreams of a lifetime seemed suddenly about to come true. She was breathtakingly lovely in her flowing white gown, but in a brief mental glimpse into half a century hence, into eternity, he knew he would feel the same about her in fifty years as he did right then. Entirely devoted, hopelessly in love, united forever.

The chaplain continued. "Who gives this woman to become this man's wife?"

"Her ma and I do." Dad let go and went to sit next to Ma.

Mary Lou whispered, "Considering it was for the president, I'll forgive you for this. But if you miss the twins' childbirth, I don't care if it's for the emperor of the universe!"

Oh, no, not another self-fulfilling prophecy! When would she learn!

The rest of the ceremony seemed a blur to Brad, and suddenly it was over.

When the chaplain abruptly said, "You may now kiss the bride," it seemed almost too soon. But he did it and willingly. She didn't even complain about his likely intense and very rank odor.

At the reception Brad finally got to meet his new mother-in-law face to face.

Dad introduced them. "Ma, you should have seen our new son in action, saving the president's life! Why dat boy ripped up the whole razor wire fence 'round Camp Davee with one hand! Dat boy walked right through a live mine-field—jes took his shoes off so they wouldn't get burnt and plowed on through! Mines exploding to the left of him. Mines exploding to the right of him. Mines explod-ing right up into his armpits, but didn't mean no more ta him than a mosquito's sneeze!

"Then practically the whole dang US Marine Corps came at him, all at once! Why dat boy wasn't about to hurt no good marines, so he just took a mighty breath and blowed 'em all down wit his hurricane wind so we could pass on through!

"Why dat boy saw de would-be killer de president 'n ran over and jes started kicking his ass, bare-handed! De killer pull out a knife 'bout two-three feet long and started slicing our boy up, but Brad he no let go till de dude be unconscious!"

"Well, you lazy ol' rascal, Pee-aire! Didn't you do nuttin' to help?"

"Matter of fact, I did. I tooks away de knife so Brad could finish kicking his ass. We did it, Ma, we saved the president's life!"

"You reckon he's a Cajun?"

"Don't rightly think so."

She turned to Brad. "Well, that's still a good job, son. Ah's mighty proud o' you! Now come gib dis ol' lady a hug an' a kiss."

Brad did so, feeling strangely ill at ease with Ma handcuffed to a policewoman, who similarly looked ill at ease, as if she would rather be anyplace other than at a joyous occasion while in the line of duty like this.

Brad whispered in Ma's ear before he let go, "Thanks for losing Crazy Joe and Billy Bupp along the way. I'm glad they didn't get here."

She beamed. "Aw, tweren't nuttin'. Jes' took me a couple o' weeks. But I knew all along dat I'd be here in time. Pa's spirit tol' me in mah dreems ever nite. I tole all y'alls 'bout dat."

She turned to Pa. "When you get here, Pee-aire, anyways?"

"Ten days ago, jes' like we planned. The chilluns picked me up at the airport. We tol' you."

"No, dat was Rougarou! I mean when you spirit return ta yo' body up'n here?"

Dad shrugged.

Mary Lou put an arm around her. "Ma, don' start dat—I mean don't start that—business again."

"Honeychile's, dis here be your real daddy. De Rougarou be gone." Ma turned to Dad, "You my real husban'. Come gimme some sugar."

Brad watched as Dad gave her a kiss that likely turned Ma's toes up.

Dad let go and beamed at Brad. "Good ol' Pee-aire. I t'ink dis ol' boy gone done gets lucky t'anight! Oo ye yi! A real Cajun homecomin' tonight! If we can free Ma from the law, that is."

Lieutenant Commander Brubake and his lovely wife, Amelia, sauntered by next.

Brad felt so happy that his friend finally got the promotion he deserved and for lack of which in recent months he had been desperately resentful and angry at Brad for getting his 0-4 first.

"Brad, you old icehole, congratulations!"

Brad smiled and shook his best man's hand. "And congratulations to you, too, my friend! Those gold oak leaves look mighty good on your shoulders! Well deserved and long overdue!"

"Brad, you know last fall when you saved us all from the dirty bombers, I was just kidding when I asked you what was next—would you save the president's life and solve the Middle East crisis. But you went and did it!"

"Well, maybe the president's life, but they haven't exactly solved the peace crisis. Just one more baby step is all."

"Still, I'm scared to predict what you might do next for fear you'll go out and do it and hurt yourself. You remember when I said you'll always be an honorary navy man to me?"

"I shore do, shipmate."

"Well, right now I have to tell you, I'm thinking you should be the next admiral. Maybe a four-star admiral of the fleet! But you'll have to change uniforms first. I'm the only one who looks at you wearing green and sees navy white. The brass will have to make it official. And you'll sure need a shower. Pee-yuu, but you stink, shipmate."

Dad grabbed Sam's hand next and shook it. "You ever see that film *Southern Comfort*?"

Brubake looked astonished. Brad rolled his eyes.

Sam moved down the line, and Amelia took Brad's hand and kissed him on the cheek. She whispered into his ear, "Thanks for everything, Brad. Sam's been getting back to normal now that his promotion finally came through. And he's cut way back on the drinking."

Brad said back in a whisper, "I'm glad, Amelia. It helps having the loving of a good woman like you."

Finally the reception was over, and one of Brad's friends attending the wedding, who was also a doctor, had a quick look at Brad's leg stab wound. The man had his medical bag in the car and stitched him up right there in the church men's room.

"It's not too deep, Brad, but it's pretty long. More of a gash than a stab. It's going to leave a pretty scar, though. You can tell your kids tall tales about how you were a swashbuckling pirate or something."

"Thanks, Walt." *Tall tales, eh? Does seem to be a family tradition.*

When he and Mary Lou headed through the tunnel of their friends and family standing on the church's front steps throwing rice and headed for their honeymoon vehicle, Brad noted with satisfaction that the only chivaree apparent was the subdued modern trend of a few cans tied to the rear bumper and simply, "Just Married," scrawled in whitewash on the rear windshield.

Man, am I glad that Crazy Joe and Billy Bupp never made it up here. Even making allowances for Dad's hyperbole, it is clear those dudes would have ruined this wedding and scandalized all my friends.

As he took the wheel and sped off, Brad noted a crazily dressed varmint of a man with torn clothes looking totally disheveled, very much as Brad himself still did. He rode on a beat-up looking bicycle with a twisted front wheelrim.

Mary Lou groaned. "Oh, no!"

Brad froze. The brood again? The ex-Stasi? There were likely members of both groups who still had it in for Brad. And he still had no idea whether they were working together against him or were separate and independent… nor how the old World War II diary may still be involved in everything.

"What is it, my beloved?" He had the sinking feeling that though this adventure had just ended and he hadn't even cleaned up from it yet, that a new one was soon to begin.

"Floor it, Brad!" she screamed. "And scrap all our honeymoon plans. We've got to change to something totally random and tell no one."

"What on earth?"

"I just saw Billy Bupp!"